DEDWADOÑT

DEDWADOÑT

PUBLISHED BY STITCHED SMILE PUBLICATIONS (THROUGH NIGHTSWAN PRESS)
© 2026 BY THOMAS R CLARK
COVER ART © 2025 BY MATT SEFF BARNES
INTERIOR DESIGN BY THOMAS R CLARK
INTERIOR PLATE ART ©2025 BY DAN HENK
ISBN: 979-8-9991091-5-6

Portions of this story were previously published in THE JOKE IS ON MANKIND © 2025.

DEDWADOÑT

"A riveting and brutal sequel to Bella's Boys" – The Voracious Gnome Reviews

EAT WITH US...

The myths and folklore of the Haudenosaunee people are as deep and rich as the soil of the land they live on. Some say their gods still watch over the People of the Longhouse. They are not wrong. Along the shores of Lake Ontario, an ancient entity indeed protects Her herd. With the lake snows comes her hunger and a desire to cull. To the Irish immigrants she is called the Cailleach, the hag who comes with the long winter. The Norse knew her to be Loki's wife, Angrboða, the mother of monsters. The people of the Seneca and Onondaga tribes call her Honyarekowa, the Great Serpent of the Genesee river...

She is all of these...

ALSO BY THE AUTHOR

GOOD BOY
THE DEATH LIST
THE GOD PROVIDES
SUMMERHOME
A PRAYER FROM THE DEAD
IMMORAL DILEMMAS
WE ARE 13

COMING SOON

THE CURSE OF KATIE ELDER
WHIRLWIND
THE WITCH OF NOVEMBER
THE TELLING OF THE BEES

DEDWADOÑT

STITCHED SMILE PUBLICATIONS
HOUSTON, TX

CONTENTS

FOR CHRISTINA, MY FAVORITE GNOME

1: EARLIER

SATURDAY, DECEMBER 14, 2024 8:00 A.M.

THE TUG HILL, REDFIELD NY

LAKE-EFFECT EVENT SNOWFALL: 4' OF ACCUMULATION

A snowmobile cuts through the north country forest and follows alongside the Salmon River, plowing through the lake-effect snowstorm. Its passenger is covered in snow, obscuring their identity. The sun rose an hour ago, but the fingers of clouds hugging the winds block much of it from the residents of Upstate New York's Tug Hill plateau. Underneath these clouds, snow falls on those unfortunate souls who have chosen to dwell there. They're a hardy folk, used to the extremes in the region's weather.

L. Frank Baum, the writer of *The Wonderful Wizard of Oz*, knew this. Born near the shores of Lake Oneida in Madison County, Baum filled the Oz stories with bits and pieces of his youth.

There's a reason the wicked old witch hails from the west. It's where the lake snows are born, and anyone who knows snow understands when you dump water on a snow bank... it liquefies. The Wicked Witch's fate is no different when Dorothy attempts to put out the fire on the hag's broom, and her glorious evil melts into a steaming puddle.

The Celtic and Gaelic peoples, who settled here during the time of the Colonizers, brought their myths and legends with them. They spoke in hushed whispers of the Cailleach, the witch who rules the Earth during fall and winter. One can assume Baum drew inspiration from this bit of folklore, as well, when creating the fantasy world of Oz. A haunted forest filled with anthropomorphic apple trees may have been the result of his imagination, as it's unlikely Baum ever experienced the terror of fleeing from an unknown threat, hidden in the snow.

The snowmobiler knows this fear, and races through the drifts, seeking any sign of civilization. The Polaris sled leaves a wake of white behind it as it charges head first into the winds. The hood of the snowsuit is tied down over the rider's head, and their hands are pulled back into the sleeves, grasping the handlebars through the elastic hem of the cuffs.

The rider scrapes a layer of ice off the fuel gauge and sees it's ticking on empty, much to the rider's chagrin. They know they won't be able to take the sled much further and gun it to go faster.

Moments later, the sled sputters and stops. "Goddamnit!" the rider shouts, identifying them as a man. His words, however, are drowned by the howling wind. He hops off the seat, and brushes the snow from his face as he looks to where he came from, seeking something.

Them... It.

Relieved to see nothing is there, he abandons the Polaris and struggles to walk through the waist-deep snow. It's a chore, one he isn't certain he can keep up, but he stays the course, knowing any other option leads to him freezing to death and ending up a human popsicle. Following the river is the best course, knowing it will bring him to people and safety.

It's not long before the winter refugee's assumptions bear fruit. A long trail of chimney smoke rises from the tree line. The plume can mean one thing... people, with a roof to repel the snow. The man moves with increased vigor, motivated by the promise of shelter from the storm... and whatever the fuck has been following him.

2: TODAY

SATURDAY, DECEMBER 14, 2024 11:40 A.M.

THE TUG HILL, REDFIELD NY

LAKE-EFFECT EVENT SNOWFALL: 3' OF ACCUMULATION (AND FALLING)

The savory scent of a boiling venison stew permeates the wilderness air. Its redolence sticks to the flying snow, as the invisible gale fights through the forest's trees. Rock music, muffled by the whipping winds, accompanies the aromas emanating from within an A-frame cabin. Near the outhouse, hanging from a thick tree limb, a trio of deer carcasses—all are gutted, and one is skinned—twist in the breeze. Occasionally they collide with one another, visually resembling giant flesh wind-chimes.

The cabin is nestled near the Salmon River Forest in Upstate New York. Isolated, it's far from the eyes of civilization. Although the snow has nearly buried the building, it's still a safe haven for brothers Joey and Aaron Hatcher. They are local hunters, members of the Onondaga Nation of the Haudenosaunee, using it as refuge from the storm. As tribal hunters, it's not the first time they've found themselves here, and it likely won't be the last.

The region is rife with unpredictable weather patterns. In particular, their current location—the westernmost edge of the Tug Hill plateau, due east of Lake Ontario—is an inclement weather magnet, and it captures snow in feet throughout the winter months. Averaging over two hundred inches of snow a year, it is one of the snowiest inhabited places in the world. This anomaly, known as lake-effect snow, can come from nothing.

Freezing Jetstream winds blow down and across the giant inland sea known as *Ontari'io* by the traditional peoples of this land. They can transform an otherwise sunny, albeit windy, day into a blizzard of white-out conditions without warning.

In spite of the weather reports indicating a possible lake-effect event, they still went hunting. Feeding their families will not wait on bad weather to pass, as they are well aware. White-tailed deer flourish in these woods. Venison has been a staple of the clan's diet for generations. The brothers are from the Onondaga's Deer clan, and can trace their lineage back to the time of Hyenwatha. The Fire Keepers of the Haudenosaunee, commonly known as the Iroquois, Onondaga translates to "People of the hills." It goes without saying the Hatcher brothers know this portion of the Adirondack Mountain range, the Tug Hill's westernmost edge, well.

"Fuckin weatherman was right. Again," Joey Hatcher says as he looks out the frosted window of the A-frame before setting the tea kettle back on the stove top.

"How much more do you think has fallen since we shoveled?" Aaron asks.

"Another dick's worth, I'd say," Joey replies.

"What kinda dick are we talkin' here? A white man's dick?"

"Okay then, two white-man dicks?" A slight giggle layers Joey's words. "Last time I opened the door to piss, I pushed a bunch out of the way and more has come since."

"So how long do you think it will last?" Aaron fidgets in his seat.

"Who knows? Weatherman said it was going to be today and tomorrow, but the bands will be shifting. We'll have to shovel again after dinner."

The interior of the cabin is an anachronism. Its decor hasn't been updated in over forty years, from the tube TV and VCR to the analog clocks, wood stove, and seventies wallpaper. Olan Mills studio family portraits, their colors still vibrant, decorate the walls. An elderly woman with thick glasses is prominent in most of them. The Stereo 8 player, part of a nearly fifty-year-old home stereo, fades the song out. An almost fifty-year-old K-Tel compilation cartridge, its title rubbed off, provides the music. The volume of the wind increases as if on cue.

A loud click from the speakers startles Joey as the stereo switches tracks, causing him to jump in his seat. The tea kettle comes to a boil on the woodstove. Steam whistles out, surprisingly in key with the music, and Joey removes it from the heat. He pours the kettle's contents into a pair of ceramic mugs.

The strings of tea bags hang over the sides, and as the water pours in, Aaron stirs his cup. A burst of wind overpowers the music—making it difficult to determine the artist playing—and causing both men to shiver.

"Stew's almost done?" Aaron asks. "It smells delicious. You used Grandmother Marion's recipe; I can tell."

"You bet your ass I did. Can't believe she's been gone over a year now," Joey says.

"I know, but she was like a hundred years old when she and Uncle RJ died."

"Yeah, and then, right after, the nursing home burned down. Right around the 2023 Windstorm."

The straight-line wind storm, or derecho, devastated the communities bordering the Great Lake's shores. Most of the region still hasn't recovered from the damage.

"It wasn't a nursing home; it was an assisted living home. And it burned down the same night as the storm. But yeah, I guess that's good. Can you see the outhouse?"

"Yeah. Why? Don't tell me you have to shit."

Aaron stands up from the folding chair as a loud, ass cheek clapping fart erupts from within his bowels. "Ayup! Gotta take a shit."

"Jesus Christ, man!" Joey wrinkles his nose in disgust. "Da fuck! You better make sure nothing slipped out into your drawers."

"Hah!" Aaron laughs, zipping up his jacket. "This is gonna suck."

"Not as bad as the stench you just released in here!"

"Oh, come on, it's not that bad!"

"You tell that to the wallpaper." Joey points to a corner of the ceiling, where a corner of the decades-old paper has peeled back.

"Really funny," Aaron chuckles, heading for the door. "Time to drop the browns off in the super bowl."

Experienced with this weather, the brothers maintain a shoveled path to their outhouse. At this point of the storm, it resembles a chasm cutting through a wall of snow. As Aaron opens the door, a gust of wind and blowing snow swirls in.

"Jesus Christ, man, close it!" Joey declares.

Aaron does so, then ventures to the outhouse, some forty yards down the path. In the conditions, it may as well be light years away.

•

A crack of thunder resonates in the sky. Icy snowflakes, propelled by thirty-mile-an-hour winds, whip along the man-made gully leading to the outhouse. It's like gnats biting at the exposed flesh on Aaron Hatcher's face and hands.

The deer they bagged yesterday, a trio of big bucks, one with a nice twelve-point rack, still hang from a line in the trees. They're safe out of the reach of any random bear not hibernating, or the packs of coy-dogs running rampant through these woods.

A tether line, supported by metal poles every ten feet, guides him to his destination. The walk isn't much of an issue, and though the new snow reaches the tops of his ankles, it's the least of his worries. He counts his steps, from the cabin to the outhouse, *one... two... three...*

With each step, Aaron's belly cramps, a result of the damn tea loosening him up. He clenches his ass cheeks, afraid the next flatulence might be solid. Or even worse... liquid. *Four... five... six...*

The idea of dying by hypothermia as a result of diarrhea doesn't mesh with Aaron's idea of a good time. *Seven... eight... nine... ten... what is that?*

He stops. A flickering ball of light, hovering in the sky and mostly obscured by the trees, illuminates the path ahead, cut by skeletal shadows.

"What the fuck is that?"

The light raises his nape hairs more than the cold's goosebumps. It's too bright to be the moon and this knowledge elevates his unease. His heart racing, he runs the rest of the way to the outhouse and shuts himself within.

With no electricity, the outhouse is dark, but for the soft glow from the ball of light shining through seams between the boards. As a result of these cracks, the walls also do nothing to keep the draft out.

The building doubles as a utility shed for their skinning and gutting tools. The brothers have kept the old traditions alive through their skills as tanners and hunters. When they were boys, their grandfathers and uncles taught them to skin and gut deer in the same manner as their people had done since before the Colonists arrived. The tools are made from antlers and bone, as well as flint, wood, and stone. These ancient implements are as effective and efficient as any modern device made of steel and plastic when it comes to dressing prey.

Aaron's teeth chatter as he unbuckles his belt and drops his jeans. Goosebumps line his legs. He sits on the ice-cold toilet seat, and lets out a surprised yelp, cursing as he does so.

"Jesus fucking Christ, that's cold."

His bowels waste no time in evacuating and relief spreads through his body. It seems solid, at least. He sighs while the wind whistles through the cracks of the outhouse. The effect creates an eerie, hypnotizing melody. Aaron hums along with the ethereal ear-worm, noting how soothing it is.

Or, it's soothing until he hears his name called from outside.

Aaron...

The voice is foreign, but familiar, one he hasn't heard in... decades?

He stops humming, holds his breath and listens, but all he hears is the wind.

"Joey, is that you? You pranking me, you dirty little bastard?"

He waits a moment for a reply, but there is none.

Aaron grabs the roll of toilet paper. He cleans himself with a few wads, drops them into the cistern, sprinkles a handful of sawdust shavings over the mess, and closes the seat after pulling his jeans back up. Another gust comes, and with it the volume of the wind's haunting song increases to a deafening level.

Aaron...

He hears his name, again, as the light disappears, the same familiar tone adding to the experience. His thoughts continue to blame his brother, *Joey and his pranks. Probably rigged the light, some speakers.*

Bundling up in his jacket, Aaron opens the door to discover the path all but obscured by thickly blowing snow. Holding the tether line, he trudges back, shielding his face from the elements with his free hand as he counts his steps.

Twenty... Twenty-one... twenty-two... He looks up, expecting to see the cabin ahead of him. *Twenty-three... twenty-four... twenty-five...*

Which he finally does. The deer carcasses are swaying in the wind, the ropes creaking. Aaron's heart jumps when something moves near the cabin.

What now? First a creepy light and now this? Whatever it is?

Whatever it is, it's no shadow, and it's outside with him in this shitty weather, on the drifts, climbing—*no skittering*—over the roof and disappearing.

What the fuck? Joey? "Joey? That you? What are you doing outside?"

There's no answer.

"Joey!" Aaron shouts, louder.

Still, there's no reply. Aaron tries again, this time shouting his brother's formal name as loud as possible.

"JOSEPH WEBSTER HATCHER!"

This time, the door flies open.

"What's your problem?" Joey asks, barely audible over the wind and music.

It's a tune Aaron can't immediately place. Trying to remember either the name of the song or who the fucking singer was, he looks around again, and sees nothing sulking in the snow.

I swear to God there was someone— something—there, he thinks. Then he calls Joey, "Hold the door, I'm coming through." Once inside, he begins removing his cold weather gear.

"Everything come out okay?" Joey asks, smirking.

"Funny." Aaron sits down at the table, where a bowl of hot venison stew awaits him. "Hey, did you hear something on the roof just now?"

"No. Why? Did you see something?"

"I dunno. Were you punking me out there?"

"Hardly. Too fuckin' cold."

"Probably just some trees moving in the wind." Aaron shrugs it off and raises the spoon to his lips, the savory steam tantalizing his tastebuds.

As he opens his mouth to take his first bite, someone—*or something*—knocks on the door.

Aaron looks at Joey, Joey looks at him, neither wishing to get up to answer.

Trees, Aaron thinks. *Wind. A branch hitting the door. That's all.*

The knocking sounds again, a distinct pattern of three in rapid succession. This time it's followed by a muffled cry.

"Hellll....."

It's clearly someone's voice, though the winds do their best to cover it up. Unsure if it's a call of distress, or a greeting, the brothers shrug in unison, push their chairs back, and stand.

Aaron's mind slips back to the skittering shadow he saw—*thought I saw, thought!*. He approaches the door with trepidation. *Is something hunting us?*

The doorknob rattles, tried from the outside. *"Helloooo?"* The voice is obviously a man's, followed by another round of rapping.

Seeing Joey has picked up one of their shotguns, holding it at the ready but not yet aiming, Aaron steps forward, grasps the knob, and turns it.

The door opens outward, and the visitor— a thick-bearded man covered in snow and ice—stands as if frozen solid, until a gust of wind blows and he collapses into the cabin's interior. The snow sticking to him explodes from his body on impact, revealing a full body snowmobile suit, but no gloves or hat.

"…help…it…it's…when…go…" The man's words drift off.

"Hey man, you okay?" Aaron asks. "What happened to you?"

The man doesn't reply. Instead, exhaling a sigh, he passes out from exposure and exhaustion.

"Holy shit. Where the fuck did he come from?" Joey asks.

"Who knows." Aaron's mind goes back to the shadow he saw—*didn't see*— climbing the A-frame.

Was it a spider? he wonders.

How could it be a spider? the logical side of his brain counters.

An octopus, then?

A snow octopus? Right!

As another flurry of wind sends a squall of snowflakes into the cabin, Aaron closes the door and locks it.

The click of the latch securing choruses with the Stereo 8 player as it switches to another track in its endless audio loop. The sound is as jarring as a gunshot.

3: YESTERDAY

FRIDAY, DECEMBER 13, 2024 10:00 A.M.

UPSTATE NEW YORK, THE SHORES OF LAKE ONTARIO

LAKE-EFFECT EVENT SNOWFALL: 6" ACCUMULATION (AND FALLING)

*T*he winds blow across the Great Lakes, picking up moisture along the way, and dropping its passenger onto the first land it hits.

Sbli'rldlnisa-aea, the elder thing, floats on these winds as they propel Her through the fingers of falling snow spreading across Her hunting grounds. Though She is far from Her lair, this is of no concern to the great goddess of ice and snow. What has She to fear from mortal beings?

An omnipresent, immortal deity, the denizens of this place cower before Her magnificent presence in awe and fear. They are Her flock to cull, or protect, on a whim. A good shepherd nurtures their charge, does it not?

Today, the great old one seeks sustenance in the maelstrom. Though Her prey is scattered, hiding within domiciles offering shelter from the elements, She will find satisfaction. After all, She's the overlord of this land and She knows the places to hunt...

They're where the snow is deepest.

•

FRIDAY, DECEMBER 13, 2024 12:36 P.M.

HILL-N-DALE COUNTRY CLUB, LOWVILLE, NY

**LAKE-EFFECT EVENT SNOWFALL: 10"
ACCUMULATION (AND FALLING)**

N early a foot of snow has fallen since the westerly winds kicked up, covering the land east of Lake Ontario in a white blanket. Though the winds roar, the humming engines of snowmobiles can be heard, the machines cutting through the terrain on treads and skis. Before the pair of sleds come into view, each of their single headlights cutting through the blowing snow, heralding their arrival. Anyone in the area witnessing them might think the snowmobiles to be cyclopean things emerging from the wilderness, with one glowing eye each.

Jason "Jay" Nichols and Stuart "Stu" Hinds love snowmobiling, but they love money more. Going out in a lake-effect event typically isn't advised, but their side job requires a bit of risk. Their wives give them grief over it, fearing for their safety being out in dangerous weather. But money talks and bullshit walks, the old adage goes. Or, in Jay and Stu's case: money takes a sled to the state park and the wives can shut the fuck up.

Each wears a backpack filled to capacity with crystal methamphetamine, the value of which is undetermined. Suffice it to say, the amphetamine made from broken down cold meds can easily transform into a metric-fuckton of money once distributed on the streets. And every time the snow falls in the off-season, Jay and Stu deliver their goods to drop off points throughout the state park system.

This exchange is so regular, they're expected when they arrive at their first destination, The Hill-N-Dale Country Club. The attached golf course is closed, of course, covered in a blanket of snow, but the local watering hole stays open for the pleasure of the local snowmobilers and ice fishermen.

It's a tradition for Stu and Jay to stop here for a little pick me up before venturing on the next leg of their ride. They know the bartender, Katie Zimmerman, a plain but attractive girl who chain smokes and gives good conversation. What they don't expect to see is another woman sitting at the bar this early in the day.

And a smoking hot one, at that.

Seeing her, they can't stop staring, memories of their wives replaced by the lust of the moment. An almond-eyed beauty with the hair of a raven, she's the epitome of beauty... from the ponytail to the fleece vest, tight sweater, stretch pants, and fur-lined faux-doeskin boots. All she's missing is a cup of pumpkin spice coffee to be a stereotype.

I bet her name is Zoe, Stu thinks.

The jukebox is playing classic rock, some song about getting laid. Could be Poison, or The Dark, or maybe Warrant. All those eighties hair metal songs sound the same, but the singer's voice is unmistakable. It's the guy from The Dark.

Brophy? Stu wonders. *Brodie?*

It really doesn't matter. What does matter is a cold adult beverage and an order of wings.

And the hot chick.

Stu is drawn to her. Brushing the snow off their suits, he and Jay remove their backpacks, gloves, and the beanies worn under their helmets. They unzip the tops of their all-weather overalls, exposing t-shirts worn underneath.

Stuart's arms are covered in faded tattoos. More ink traces its way up his neck. He reaches the bar first as the song fades out, making sure to sit closest to the woman. Jay joins him.

Katie has already secured a pair of pint glasses. "You know how I knew I'd see you guys today?" she asks as she fills a glass with Labatt Blue.

"I don't know, tell us." Stu replies.

Katie points to the bay window overlooking the golf course, "The snow is falling."

"Well, duh. It's what we do," Jay says. "Snow falls, we ride. Wouldn't you?"

"Yeah," she agrees. "The usual?"

"Sure," Stu says, "Use that ghost pepper honey. I love that shit."

"The Frog's Point stuff? I think we have some left."

"Yer gonna shit fire balls," Jay quips. Stu punches him in the shoulder.

"A'ight. You two behave. I'll be right back." Katie disappears into the kitchen.

"Behave? I mean, what could we possibly do?" Stu laughs.

The bar television is tuned to the weather, the signal from the satellite choppy and making the picture pixelated. The weather girl, a buxom and voluptuous blonde, is pointing to the fingers of lake snow drifting off Lake Ontario, warning that feet of it could be possible in some portions of the Tug Hill.

Stu takes a healthy draught of his beer, jeering the meteorologist's prediction of a snowpocalypse, and turns to the woman sitting next to them. "And who might you be?

Other than gorgeous, that is. Let me guess. Zoe, right?"

"He shoots... he misses. Sorry, tiger. The government calls me Sandy Bellavia. But you can call me Bella." She sips from a cup of steaming hot tea.

"Okay then, Bella it is. I'm Stu, this is Jay. So, what brings a doll like you out here on a day like this?"

"The same thing as you."

"Is that so?"

"It is. I love the snow, among other things."

"And what could those things be?" Stu says, swiveling his barstool so his knee brushes the woman's leg. He moves his hand near hers. At the touch of his fingertips, he feels a jolt like a static shock, and recoils.

"Things your wife wouldn't approve of, I would think?" Bella says, glancing at his wedding band.

"Rings don't fill no holes, ain't that right Stu?" Jay claps him on the back.

"That's a fact," Stu concurs and tips his glass. "Who wants to make naked snow angels today?"

Bella does not join their laughter. She turns away, moving her leg away from Stu and putting the back of her stool to him.

"What? We're just joking," he protests.

"I'm not."

"No need to be a prude, squaw bitch." Stu says, his smile turning into a scowl.

Bella stirs her tea, brow furrowed.

"Hey, now. That's uncalled for." Katie says as she returns to her station behind the bar. "What did I say about behaving?"

"What? Call a spade a spade, right?" Stu takes another long draught off his pint glass, emptying half of it.

"Jesus Christ, Stu! You're annoying my only other customer. For fuck's sake, man." Katie makes eye contact with Bella and mouths the words *I'm sorry.*

"We weren't doing nothing wrong, just having some fun," Stu says, then decides to up the ante by invoking the owner. "Doc wouldn't give us a hard time about it."

"Doc's not here. When I'm behind the bar, this is my place, and he'd tell you the same. Now, the two of you can move to different seats, or you can leave and not come back. This is *my* bar, not your pal's, when I'm behind the counter. Don't you forget that, Mr. Hinds. Doc'll tell ya the same thing."

"Yadda yadda yadda. Whatever." Stu says.

But he and Jason move to a table, finishing their beers and not asking for refills. Outside of the TV and the music, the room is silent.

When Katie returns to the kitchen, Stu glares at Bella, then looks at Jay. "Fuck this place. Let's go."

"What about our wings?"

"She can stick them up her ass for all I'm concerned. Telling us what to do, like she thinks she owns this place."

Jay chews his lip in hesitation, then nods. They zip up their suits, and put their backpacks and gear back on. The woman at the bar watches them out of the corner of her eye. As they leave, Stu turns back just long enough to flip her a middle-finger before the door closes.

•

Katie feels the vibration of her phone in the ass pocket of her jeans. She fishes it out, checks the screen, smiles, and answers, setting it to speaker so she can finish preparing the double order of wings.

"Hello, you," she says.

"Hey baby. Is he there?"

"Is my husband ever here when I'm working?" Katie says.

"You never know," Doc Coyne replies. "What's the till look like?"

"It's been slow, and with a big lake-effect on the way, who knows? We might get snowed in." She lets her voice slip into an alluring, sensual tone. "Have to huddle together for warmth."

"Oh, that would be awful. I might have to stop by, keep you company. Just in case."

"I think I'd like that," Katie says, adding a dollop of hot honey to the sauce mix.

"I figured you would. You know what I'd like?"

"Whatever might that be?" she asks coyly, as she dumps the wings in the bowl and shakes them. The ancient Tupperware container, seasoned by years of use, thrums like a drum as the chicken pieces collide.

"My cock in your mouth," Doc says in a sexy growl.

"Oh yeah? You know what else I would like?"

"What's that?"

"Your load in my mouth and your cock in my pussy." She's getting wet at the thought.

"I think we can arrange that, especially if it's slow."

"I like it slow." Katie drags out the 'oh' and puts the wings in a basket, adding the garnishments, complete with celery and carrot sticks and bleu cheese.

"I know you do, baby."

"I gotta go," she tells him. "Order of wings to serve up."

"A'ight. I'll be down in a few hours."

"You bet your ass you will."

•

S itting at the bar stool wearing a skin from The Others, sipping on her drink, Bella—otherwise known as Sandy Bellavia, or by the names given to Her by the ancient peoples, names such as Sbli'rldlnisa-aea, Honyarekowa, or Angrboða—watches the irritated men bundle up and exit the Hill-N-Dale.

Still troubled by what occurred when She attempted to touch one, Bella looks at Her blistered fingertips, the scent of the burning flesh still hanging in the air.

The goddess readies Her avatar to follow them, then She overhears Katie's phone conversation. Curiosity leads Her to sit back down... and listen.

Not all those She preys upon are men...

•

When Katie returns with the wings, Stuart and Jason are gone. She can hear the engines of their snowmobiles as they speed away.

"Those bastards!" She sets the basket on the bar, and sighs in exasperation, then turns to address her remaining customer. "I'm sorry they were such shitheads—"

No one is there. The previously occupied barstool is empty. Even the jukebox has fallen silent.

Fine, whatever.

Dismissing it, Katie heads to the rest room to freshen up before Doc arrives. With the incoming snowstorm, she anticipates receiving a considerable amount of plowing.

•

In the stall, she rubs herself a little, thinking about Doc fucking her with his giant cock. For fifteen years of marriage, she dealt with disappointment in the bedroom for the sake of the kids. Just her luck to get knocked up by the guy with the smallest dick. Who, of course, would also be the one to step up to the plate, do the honorable thing, and marry her.

Now, three kids later, Chris's cock was no bigger, making Katie no happier.

Until, that is, Doc and his trouser monster. She'd accidentally bumped her ass against his crotch, squeezing past him behind the bar on a busy night. The feel of such a bulge through the denim instantly set off her lust.

As soon as the last of the stragglers had finally headed for home, Doc was pounding her cunt with a massive jackhammer of ecstasy. For the first time in years, Katie went to bed happy and sexually satisfied.

She can hardly wait for him to get here. Hopefully, the storm would keep everyone else away, and they'd be able to go at it as much as they liked.

The jukebox, suddenly coming to life again at maximum volume, startles her out of her lewd train of thought. A heavy metal party riff resonates through the bar. It's more of The Dark, and their dirty little song about the guitarist's foot fetish, S.O.M.F.

But who the hell cranked it up to eleven? Is that Bella chick still here after all? Or did someone else wander in?

Katie rushes to finish her bathroom break. Of course, she just *would* need to shit, on top of everything else. And, of course, it *would* have to be an epic bowel movement, her butt working overtime.

Then, also of course, when she finally feels like she's done, it's a whole new can of worms when she wipes.

Each wad of paper comes out with more streaks of crap on it than the previous. *What am I? A human shit crayon?* Katie wonders.

She goes through nearly an entire roll of toilet paper before she's clean. She flushes, washes her hands, dries them, opens the door to exit the lavatory...

And the music stops right in the middle of the song.

"What the hell?" Katie says, nervously playing with the pop-up on her phone.

She notes the bar is still empty. The aroma of freshly cooked and tossed wings makes her belly grumble. Through the windows she can see the snow falling in such magnitude, it obscures her view of the forest and hills.

A pulsating pink and purple light from outside catches Katie's attention. It's nothing like the lights from a car, not even the red-and-blue kind they had on patrol cars.

Could things get any weirder?

Stepping to the door, she opens it and looks to see what might be making the light. As she does, a wall of snow pelts her, covering the front of her body in a layer of icy flakes. She winces as it stings her face and eyes.

"Jesus Christ!" Katie exclaims. She shakes her head, paws snow from her eyes, looks again, and blinks, uncertain of what she's seeing.

There appears to be a giant tree trunk, as big around as an ancient oak, in the middle of the driveway, where no tree was an hour ago. But it pulses with light and color, shifting through paisley shades of blues, purples, and pinks.

Is it a tree? If it is, where did it come from? Trees don't just sprout up that fast! And why is it glowing?

She raises her gaze, moving up the trunk. Through the blowing snow, she sees not boughs and branches, but a mass of squirming tentacles and tendrils. Fumbling with her phone, she struggles to open its camera app to take video. Before she can, a tendril whips down and flicks the phone out of her hand. It lands inside the doorway.

Come to Us!

A voice screams inside Katie's head. Frozen in place, shivering as much from fear as the cold, she pisses herself, despite having been to the bathroom mere moments ago.

Come... to... US!

A pair of the shifting purplish tentacles shoot toward her. Katie screams as rows of suckers lined with serrated teeth bite into her flesh. Wrapping around her arms and shoulders, the tentacles lift her into the air. Her feet kick as she thrashes about, trying fruitlessly to free herself from the terrible grip. Blood drips down her legs, spotting the fresh snow with crimson pellets.

Then the tentacles retract, pulling her with them. The sudden flying tug reminds her of the time she and Chris rode the Himalaya at the fair, when they started dating. The collective screams of all the passengers on that long-ago ride paled in comparison to the shrill screech coming out of her mouth at this very moment.

Her ear-piercing shriek ends abruptly, as the thing in the snow consumes Katie Zimmerman, absorbing her within its trunk and tentacles. The ambient silence of blowing wind follows.

4: THEN...

STÖÐ, ICELAND, 806 A.D.

A wide river narrows into a vast fjord next to an Iron Age village of wooden longhouses on the coast of the Atlantic ocean. Named Stöð, after the river, the residents have lived here for a decade now, carving out a new life. The setting sun casts a haze of fiery orange over the horizon, popping out behind the craggy mountain tops and smoking volcanic peaks further inland. A dozen dragon ships with their sails furled are moored in the docks.

Within the confines of a stable, hidden behind livestock, stalls, and bales of hay, Ólafur Sigurðsson and Freydís Hildasdottir fuck. Their clothing discarded, the two naked bodies blend together as one in the shadows. Their lust guides them as Ólafur thrusts into Freydís. Propelled by his pelvis, Ólafur's cock is a smith's hammer, forging steel. It's furious and passionate, and though it's the middle of winter, they are covered in a sheen of sweat, and steam rises off their bodies.

Ólafur tenses up, and grabs Freydís by the throat as they climax in unison. Sighs and moans slip from them as they collapse onto the straw.

"Do you still love me?" Freydís asks.

"Of course," Ólafur replies.

"You will talk to the Jarl tomorrow?"

"If not tomorrow, the next day." He draws a sheepskin across them, covering their naked bodies. "It depends on how busy he is. We don't want to bother him with trivial nonsense."

"Our love is nonsense? If that's the case, then I must tell you now."

"Tell me what?"

"I'm with child."

"You're what?" Ólafur's head tilts. "How?"

"How? You ask me how, after what we just did? So, you must talk to the Jarl tomorrow; it cannot wait. And... my mother knows."

"Your mother?!" He sits up, frustration growing on his face.

"She noticed I haven't had my blood. I can't lie to her."

He groans. "Freydís, you don't understand!"

"What don't I understand?"

"What we've done is against the laws of the gods and the people!"

"But love doesn't care about the laws of men or the gods. Don't you remember telling me so?"

"You foolish, silly girl! I told you what I told you to bed you, and nothing more. "

"But... love!"

"Love?" He pushes her aside and stands. "You ruined that."

"What about the child?"

"What about it? How can I be sure it's mine?"

She gasps at Ólafur's reply as he pulls on his clothes.

"As of now," he goes on, "I don't know you. And as for this?" He kicks her in the belly, causing her to fold into a fetal position, holding her gut. "It's not mine."

"Ólafur!" Freydís screams as he stalks out of the stable. "Ólafur!"

He ignores her, storming away without another word.

She pulls the sheepskin up to her face and weeps.

•

Auður rushes gladly to her husband's arms. He holds her tight and she notices he's covered in sweat from his chores. His demeanor appears sour, so she smiles, hoping it will brighten his disposition.

"You've worked hard today, husband." She mops his brow with the sleeve of her dress.

"Aye, and now I would like to feast and sleep."

"I have a hearty stew of mutton prepared on the hearth."

"My dutiful wife. Come, let's go before we are delayed by anyone. I've had my fill of people for the day."

Hand in hand, Ólafur and Auður head to their home.

•

Auður is woken from a deep sleep by a pounding on the door. She sits up to see her husband is already awake, and dressed, an axe in his hand. "What is it?" she asks. "Who's here? What is happening?"

"They're here for me," Ólafur says grimly.

"What? Who? Why?"

"The Jarl's men, and over the lies of a stable slut, I'm sure."

"Stable slut? Freydís?"

"You can't tell me you haven't seen it. She lusts after me as well as all the men in the village. Now she claims she's with child, and the fingers pointed at me."

Auður gasps. "Why at *you*, Ólafur?"

"Because I am often at the stables, and idle tongues make gossip."

The pounding on the door intensifies, accompanied by raised voices demanding entry. Ólafur secures his shield, and stands ready, his axe at hand. When the door bursts open, members of the Jarl's personal guard step in.

"Ólafur Sigurðsson, you stand accused," Áki Jónsson, the Jarl's hersir, declares.

Behind the men, next to her mother, stands Freydís. "It is him!" she says, loud and clear and defiant.

Ólafur rushes forward, raises his axe and strikes the first guard, his childhood friend Eiríkr Hansen. The blade sinks into his former friend's shoulder and the man cries out in pain. Halfdan Fisker, the next guard, takes advantage of the confusion and tackles Ólafur, driving the man to the ground. He drops his shield and loses the grip on his axe in the process. Eiríkr kicks him in the head, and the dazed Ólafur stops resisting.

Within moments, the guards have Ólafur in their custody.

Auður pummels at Áki's chest with her bare fists, but her blows do nothing. "He is innocent!" Auður sobs.

Hilda Bjornsdottir, mother of Freydís, scoffs. "Tell that to the baby in my child's belly!"

"The Jarl will determine if he is or not," Áki says. "And after what he's done to Eiríkr, I doubt the Jarl will be lenient."

"The Jarl will send him to the Móðir, where he belongs!" Freydís crows.

Auður shudders at the suggestion. "No! You can't do that! You are damning him to those cultists if you do! You can't do this! Banish him instead! Please! Banish him!"

"Perhaps Ólafur should've thought of this before he plowed another girl's field. If the Jarl decrees it to be so, then he will meet the Móðir. Cry to the Alföðr all you like, but I doubt Óðinn will hear you. Haven't you already figured out he doesn't care about the affairs of men, or women?" Áki pushes her aside.

She weeps as the guards disappear with her unconscious husband. The guards ignore her pleas. "Alföðr guide me!" Auður cries, until she realizes what she must do... and who she must talk to. One must fight a god with a god, no?

She knows she must go into the wild, and consult with the Lang-amma.

5: YESTERDAY

FRIDAY, DECEMBER 13, 2024 1:47 P.M.

WHETSTONE GULF STATE PARK, LOWVILLE, NY

LAKE-EFFECT EVENT SNOWFALL: 17" ACCUMULATION (AND FALLING)

The sleds barrel through the frozen drifts. Skis and treads propel Stu and Jay forward until a squall rises, blotting out everything in a brief white-out and causing the men to stop.

They are on a ridge alongside Route 26. Idling his Arctic-Cat ZR-9000, Jay raises the face shield on his helmet. Sitting on his Polaris PRO RMK, Stu does the same, freeing his beard. Within seconds, snow turns its dark brown to white.

"Man, you already look like Santa," Jay says.

"That must make you my elf," Stu replies.

"I thought that was the girl at the bar."

Stu raises a gloved middle finger.

They peer down the gully toward their destination. With the heavy snowfall, and the forecast calling for more, any tracks they might leave behind would quickly be covered over. It means they can take the proper path, rather than risking fallen logs, wire fencing, or other obstacles by navigating the slope.

"Let's do this," Stu says. "I want to get back home before dark."

"Relax, we have plenty of time," Jay assures him. "Sun don't go down until 4:30 and your old lady isn't going nowhere."

"Yeah, yeah, yeah, I know. I'm just tired of this snow already, and winter is only just starting." As something catches his attention, he points, adding, "Hey, what's that?"

Near the ranger station, a trio of floating lights slowly dance in the wind, crackling and flickering. They're weird in color, shifting through pinks, purples, and blues.

"Ball lightning, maybe?" Jay suggests, revving his Arctic Cat. "Let's find out, cos that's where we're going anyway!"

Stu pulls his face plate down. Jay follows suit. The sleds roar to life and descend toward the road, passing the sign marking the entrance to the Whetstone Gulf State Park.

By the time they arrive at the ranger station, the psychedelic lights have disappeared, so they don't stop to look, heading instead for the cabins further into the park.

Seeing something ahead, Stu slides his snowmobile to a stop, kicking up a wall of snow.

"What's wrong?" Jay asks, also stopping.

Stu can barely hear him through the helmet and over the engines. He points to what he saw, but there's nothing there.

"What the fuck?" he says. "I swear I saw a deer."

"So? We must've scared it off."

"Yeah, I guess." Stu inches forward, scanning the snowy terrain. "Hey, there it—"

The furry lump, almost buried in the fresh snow, is the body of a black bear. Its rib cage is ripped open, strands of ruddy flesh and muscle hanging off the bony spikes.

The discovery of a dead bear in and of itself isn't all that bad a thing. What disturbs them is that there's *also* a deer, a white-tailed deer with its head buried in the bear's eviscerated belly. Its antlers scrape on the bear's exposed ribs.

"What the fuck?" Stu blurts in shock, his eyes wide.

The deer raises its head. Much of the skin and hair on its face is missing, revealing patches of skull. Strings of sinew hang from its mouth.

"Holy shit," Jay says. "It's like a wendigo!"

"A what?"

"One of them Indian cannibal spirit things. Makes people eat each other."

"Are you shitting me?"

"No, man, they say it looks like a fuckin' deer! A half-dead zombie deer, like this fuckin' thing!"

The deer snorts as if in response, steam billowing from its disfigured snout.

"That's crazy."

"Look at it!" Jay insists. "Shit, Stu, it's a monster! We're fucked!"

"Monster? I'll show you how we deal with monsters." Stu pulls a .30-.06 Springfield from its sheath alongside his seat on the Polaris.

"You can't kill a wendigo that way!"

"I can't?" Stu briefly pictures the woman from Hill-N-Dale, thinking, *Buh-bye biotch!* as he squeezes the trigger.

The gun barks fire and thunder. The back of the deer's head explodes in a splatter of blood, bone, and brain. Its body takes a moment to realize it's dead, then collapses atop the bear, staining the snow in shades of red.

Smoke wafts from the barrel. Stu and Jay sit in silence, waiting for further movement.

There is none.

"Wendigos," Stu scoffs. "Monsters. Indian legends. Zombie deer. Bullshit." He re-sheaths the rifle. "A starving animal will eat anything. Don't be a superstitious pussy. Now, let's get a move on. I want to get home before dark."

•

As the snowmachines depart, a trio of pulsating lights emerge from the tree line. Rising into the blowing snow, they swirl about, hovering over the bodies of the dead bear and deer.

A substance drips from the lights, black with thick, viscous strands, pulsating as gravity draws it down. The ichor lands on the corpses, bubbling and spitting. Each burst releases a thousand whispers, hidden in the wind's roar, as the substance spreads across the carcasses.

The lights race away into the wind. After a moment, when their soft glow disappears into the blowing snow, something happens.

If Stuart or Jason had witnessed it, they surely would have gone mad. Stu's learning experience would be a crash course in how ineffective a rifle is against "whatever the fuck" he saw. And Jay? He'd likely be screaming "WENDIGO!"

You see, this is because the bodies of the bear, and deer... well, They stir, and rise from the snowpack. They move with a stiff, trembling gait, along the trail left behind by the snowmobiles.

'foll…ow,' *the bear grunts, its vocal cords unsure of how to articulate human language.*

'yessssss…' *the deer replies, with what's left of its brain pan suffering the same dilemma.*

'Sbli'rldlnisa-aea, Gudinnen av alle ting,' *They sing together, in the first language They learned. They sing to Their 'goddess of all things…'* Sbli'rldlnisa-aea *for* himmelens droning.'

Jason and Stuart will have plenty of time to question reality and scream later, when The Others catch up to Their Mistress and Her chosen prey.

·

FRIDAY, DECEMBER 13, 2024 3:37 P.M.

HILL-N-DALE COUNTRY CLUB, LOWVILLE, NY

LAKE-EFFECT EVENT SNOWFALL: 19" ACCUMULATION (AND FALLING)

Three hours pass before another person arrives at the country club. A white truck, a Ford F-150, its suspension jacked up and chains on the tires, stops at the edge of the parking lot. It's near zero visibility and the Ford is nearly camouflaged by the falling snow. A yellow plow blade and lights betray the obfuscated vehicle.

With its headlights piercing the twilight darkness of dusk and falling snow, Doc Coyne guns the F-150 into the Hill-N-Dale's parking lot. Built for this climate, the truck barrels in and drops the blade. An explosion of snow erupts as the steel does its job.

After a few more passes, clearing out a majority of the parking lot, he comes to a stop next to Katie Zimmerman's KIA. The cherry red Sportage is buried in a foot of snow. No other cars or snowmobiles can be seen. This pleases him. "I've got you all to myself," he says, and a lecherous smile covers his face. The ED pills are kicking in, and he can feel his trouser snake coming to life.

Doc steps out of his truck and heads to the door, surprised to find over a foot of snow has fallen where Katie shoveled the walk and area around the front. Stepping into this area, he discovers a layer of pink slush under the fresh snow. It's ankle deep and reeks of sickly sweet rot.

"The fuck is this?" he says, curling his nose, and wonders if they have a sewage issue. Thoughts of plowing Katie with his cock are starting to fade.

Stepping inside the entrance, his foot connects with something solid on the foyer's floor. It skips across the tiles and bangs into the step separating the entrance from the club. He bends over and picks it up. A cell phone, and judging from the case, it's Katie's. He continues in and is greeted with warmth and silence.

"Katie? Where ya at? I came down to plow the lot. I found your phone." There's no reply. He adjusts his cock in his pants and looks around the back of the bar. No one is there. "Katie? Hello? Is anyone here?" There are no answers.

Doc lights a smoke and sets about searching the building. The kitchen is empty. Peeking his head into the ladies room, there's nothing. With the exception of himself, the country club is empty. "What the fuck?" He scratches his head, and while bewildered, pours himself a glass of Jameson on the rocks, and slams it back.

The bar's landline phone rings. Doc answers.

"Hill-N-Dale. Doc speaking."

"Hi Doc," the woman on the other end of the line says. "This is Sarah Hinds. My husband, Stu, is he there?"

"No, no one is here, Sarah. He might've been earlier, but my bartender isn't here, either, so I can't ask her if she saw him or not."

"Okay, that's weird. He should have been home by now, and I knew he was stopping by your place."

"The weather is getting bad. He may have held out in a shelter somewhere. Was he alone?"

"No. Jay Nichols was with him, and his wife is worried, too. If you see them, can you please ask them to call us?"

"That I can do. You stay safe in the storm, and have a good night."

"You, too." As soon as Doc hangs up, Katie's cell phone comes to life, startling him. "What do we have here?"

A pop-up alert opens, and Doc sees it is a message from Katie's husband, Chris: *WHY CAN'T YOU ANSWER ME? IT'S BEEN HOURS!* He notices a chain of alerts going back a few hours. Another message hits as he's reading. *I READ THE TEXTS! I KNOW!* The alert declares.

The outside windows light up from another vehicle entering the parking lot at a high rate of speed.

"Son of a bitch," Doc says as he watches the truck, a black Dodge, eponymously ram into the side of his F-150. The crack of the impact is loud, rattling the windows and door of the country club. The door of the Dodge flies open and Chris Zimmerman jumps out, something long grasped in his hand. Doc runs behind the bar and grabs the baseball bat they keep there as an equalizer.

The door bursts open and Chris enters the country club. Snow covers his person, but it doesn't hide the .12 gauge shotgun in his hands. "Where is she?" His words are slurred, and he reeks of booze.

"Not here?" Doc replies, keeping the bar between him and Chris, a white-knuckle grip on the bat's handle.

"I think she is. And ya know why?"

"Tell me."

"First off, her SUV is out there. Second, she was on the fucking schedule today. And when she's on the schedule, you aren't here, unless it's busy... and guess what Doc? It's fuckin dead. So why are you here? Oh, I know why!" He chambers a round into the shotgun and discharges it into the ceiling, blowing a hole in it.

Doc grasps the back of the bar and grits his teeth. "Easy now, Chris. I came here to plow and found Katie, well, I didn't find her, cos she disappeared."

"That's bullshit and you know it. Wanna hear something funny? Last week I went through the phone bills. And do you know what I found?"

"I don't know. Paper mites?"

"Real funny, motherfucker. Yer a regular old comedian." Chris charges the shotgun and points it at Doc. "I read the texts, Doc. You can't lie your way out of it. I know you've been fucking her."

"Take it easy, man. You don't want to do this."

"Where is she? Is she back there?"

"I told you, I don't know where she is. Put the gun down, man. Think about your kids."

"I did. That's why they're at my Mom's..." he pauses, staring off at nothing, until he twitches. "Where the fuck is she hiding, Doc?" Chris tries to stretch his neck out, to get a look behind the bar and into the kitchen.

He loses his balance and tips over, falling on the floor and pulling the trigger. The shotgun roars and the mirror, along with a dozen liquor bottles behind the bar, explodes. Shattered glass flies everywhere.

Now or never, Doc decides. He runs to the edge of the bar, the bat grasped in his fist. He rounds the corner to see Chris, sitting on the floor, aiming the shotgun at him.

"Fuck you!" Doc screams and rears the bat back to swing at Chris's head.

"You stupid fuck, bringing a bat to a skeet shoot," Chris replies, and unloads the shotgun into Doc. "Buh bye, biotch!" he screams over the thunder of the weapon discharging.

Five .12 gauge shells impacting a human body in succession, and within a matter of seconds, is devastating. The first blast turns Doc's groin into hamburger, and blows his still hard dick off. This causes Doc to drop the bat, and grab the void between his legs. The wound is what ultimately kills him, except he doesn't know it yet.

A target frozen in place, none of the remaining shells pass through his body. Instead they pulverize the rib bones, muscle, and fat of his torso into a pink puree, covering his exposed sternum. The concussive force of the impacts push Doc back into the bar, allowing him to maintain a vertical base.

Held up by the polished mahogany, Doc has a moment to stare in awe at the sucking chest wounds covering his chest, and marvel at how much the bar's interior now resembles a butcher's shop, or a club post a GWAR concert. He gasps for breath as he chuckles, until a click breaks him out of his stupor.

"If you're here Katie, and I know you are somewhere, I love you, our kids love you!" Chris Zimmerman shouts, slurring his words, tears in his eyes. "But you had to go and fuck him, didn't you? Well guess what, you stupid bitch? Now you don't get either of us, and my Mom gets the kids!"

Doc listens to Chris's suicide rant, and raises his eyes to witness his murderer swallowing the barrel of the shotgun. He says nothing... feels nothing... can do nothing... but watch the man squeeze the trigger.

When Chris's brains blow out, covering the drop ceiling, Doc finds it funny how the brains splattering into the tiles resembles caviar being shot out of a garden hose. He chokes a laugh at the thought one last time, aspirates, and dies.

6: TODAY

SATURDAY, DECEMBER 14, 2024 12:35 P.M.

THE TUG HILL, REDFIELD NY

LAKE-EFFECT EVENT SNOWFALL: 4' OF ACCUMULATION

Aaron and Joey wipe the remaining snow off the stranger's unconscious body. When they pull his overalls off, taking his t-shirt along with it, they see his torso is covered with tattoos. The majority are tribal-like runes, while many others are clearly Norse. Valknuts, troll crosses, raven and wolf heads, Vegvísir (the compass), the Helm of Awe, and the thunder god Þórr's hammer, Mjǫllnir, are the most prevalent.

Aaron pats him down for any possible identification and discovers there is none. Whoever he is, the man is built like a brick shithouse. They drag him to the old sofa—he weighs at least 250 pounds—heave him up onto it, and cover him with a couple of blankets.

"Who do you think he is?" Joey asks as they return to the table.

"Fuck if I know. Some stupid tourist out snowmobiling in the woods when he shouldn't be."

"When he wakes up, we'll find out."

"For sure. I don't like waiting."

"Grow some patience, big brother. It's not like he's gonna do anything sleeping on the couch," Joey says.

Aaron chews his lip and shrugs. He goes to the old Frigidaire and grabs a cold Labatt Blue. "You want one?"

"Sure," Joey replies.

They resume eating their stew. The music from the Stereo-8 begins to garble. Then the tape snaps, and a high-pitched whine follows.

"Well, that sucks. I thought these things lasted forever," Aaron says.

Joey pops out the busted cartridge and replaces it with a bright red one. One of ABBA's many radio hits, 'Take A Chance on

Me,' is in mid-song—highlighting the vocal harmonies of Frida, Benny, Agnetha and Björn. It's an inescapable earworm.

"Aw fuck, are you kidding me? I'm gonna have this song in my head all day," Joey says. "We really should label these."

"There's fates worse than ABBA. It coulda been that damn blue one," Aaron says.

"What, Barry Manilow's greatest hits?" Joey laughs. "Come on, that was Grandmother Marion's favorite."

"I swear she thought she was Lola dancing at the Copacabana."

Their guest stirs.

"Uhhhh..." His eyes flutter as he attempts to open them. "Where ... where am I?"

He rolls off the couch and lands on the floor with a loud thud, jarring the Stereo-8 into changing tracks with its typical 'click.' Another ABBA song, 'Waterloo,' comes to life while the Hatchers rush to the stranger's aid, assisting him back onto the sofa.

"Who... who are you?" he asks, rubbing his shoulder.

"We'd like to know the same about you," Aaron says. "You showed up at our door—".

He jerks and gasps. "Wendigo!"

Joey and Aaron exchange a look, and burst out laughing.

"Yeah. I know it sounds crazy, but you've got to believe me! A wendigo is out there! It came after me and my buddy. It got him! Fucking *ate* him!"

"So, let me get this straight," Aaron says, bringing himself under control with an effort. "A wendigo, a made-up fantasy thing, ate your friend?"

"Right in front of me. Bones and all."

"Yeah?" Joey asks, sounding skeptical. "So then how did you escape?"

"This, I think?" He touches a Þórr's hammer charm hanging from a silver chain around his neck. "It touched me with one of its tentacles, I felt some sort of ... shock, like static electricity? And it ran away. Or disappeared. Whatever."

"What did you say your name was?" Aaron asks.

"I didn't. But it's Stu. Stuart Hinds."

"Well, Stuart Hinds," Joey says, "I'm Joe Hatcher and this is Aaron, my brother. This friend of yours—"

"Jay."

"Jay," Joey agrees, nodding. "Why do you think a wendigo, something that doesn't exist—"

"It's goddamn *real*, I tell you!"

"Let me guess, it had antlers and fangs."

"No, that was the deer," Stuart says, aggravated. "This was different. I can't describe it. It was all weird colors, and it had tentacles, and—"

"Tentacles?" Aaron echoes, recalling the spiderlike shadowy something he thought he saw a while ago, skittering over the A-frame's roof.

"Yes, *tentacles*!" Stuart nearly shouts.

Aaron and Joey exchange another glance.

"Where were you when this happened?" Joey asks.

"Whetstone Gulf."

"Dude, really?" Aaron shakes his head. "That's thirty miles away, overland; fifty by car. And in this weather? You should be a popsicle."

"No shit. I drove my sled all night through the snow. Ran out of gas near here." Stu shifts on the couch, holds his belly, and grimaces. "Do you have a bathroom? I need to go."

"If you gotta number one, then step outside the door," Aaron tells him. "If it's a number two, well, all we have is the outhouse; you'll have to suit up."

"Where's the outhouse?"

"Just outside. Follow the trench, There's a tether, too."

"And don't mind our kills," Joe adds. "They aren't wendigos, I promise."

"Real funny," Stu grumbles, getting into his gear. "I know what I saw."

And we know wendigos don't exist, Aaron thinks, but keeps it to himself. *Same as cursed Indian burial grounds and Medicine Men.*

As Stuart steps outside into the elements, ABBA's Greatest Hits changes tracks again. This time it's back to 'Take a Chance on Me.'

•

Redskins? *Really?* Stu wonders as he sits on the makeshift toilet. *Where the fuck have I ended up?*

Hanging along the outhouse walls are various implements used for hunting, skinning, butchering, tanning, and God knows what all else. He sees sharpened antlers, pieces of rock and glass wrapped in twine, a stretched deer skin pinned up like caveman art.

He wishes he still had his rifle. Then he could let these Indians know who was the boss around here. But no, he'd left it behind.

Did I really kill a wendigo?

He disregards the thought, which is hard to do with the peculiar decor of the outhouse staring back at him.

It was a deer, nothing but a deer, he reminds himself.

Another inner voice speaks up, sounding eerily like Jay. *If it was just a fucking deer, which you shot before and blew half its head off, then how was it still up and walking around? And the bear, let's not forget the bear, which you know damn well was dead!*

Stu doesn't have any answers. Utter fear and confusion were, ultimately, why he'd fled the cabin in Whetstone Gulf.

Well, that, and the explosion, and whatever the fuck ate Jay. How the hell am I going to explain it to his wife? Not to mention the Reapers?

Stu wipes his ass and doesn't bother to sprinkle any wood shavings on it. Why should he? It's not like it will solve anything. An idea strikes him as he's zipping up. He takes one of the antler knives from the wall and thumbs the blade. Nice and sharp. It's a little insurance policy in case the redskins need to be dealt with. He's sure it will gut an Indian just as well as it eviscerates a deer.

As he emerges from the outhouse, blowing snow   obscures his vision. He takes hold of the guideline and starts for the cabin.

And is greeted by a blinding flash of light as something strikes him in the back of the head, sending his thoughts to the void.

7: THEN...

STÖÐ, ICELAND 806 A.D.

Standing outside the entrance to a volcanic cave, Auður shakes in fear. The torch in her grip spits sizzling embers onto the snow-covered rocks. It's little more than a dormant magma tunnel, but what resides inside may have the answers she seeks.

Coming here is a last resort, and could end with her own dedeath. But she doesn't care. Without her husband, she will be an outcast in the village. Unless she can find another man in need of a wife, she's likely bound to be reduced to a beggar or a whore.

For Auður, none of these are appealing options. If the Norns have truly woven such as her fate, she intends to change the stitch.

The cave mouth is intricately carved with knots and runes. Smoke issues from the nostrils of a giant wolf's head sculpted at its apex. A sulphury odor fills the air. The hairs raise on her nape and arms, but she cannot let it stop her from entering the lair of the Lang-amma.

Auður holds the torch before her as she makes her way into the tunnel. A soft chanting can be heard, growing in volume the deeper she descends into the bowels of the earth.

Eventually, she reaches a chamber, where a bearded old man and a young woman sit cross-legged before a small hearth. They are both naked, painted with runes.

"Who dares enter the lair of the Lang-amma?" intones the man, without moving.

"I am Auður. I come under the protection of Óðinn Alföðr and Þórr Hlödynson!" Auður touches an amulet featuring Mjölnir, Þórr's hammer, adorning her bosom.

"And you risk the Lang-amma's wrath by coming here? You know her tithe, as all do. A soul for a soul. Tell us your purpose."

"I seek the knowledge to slay the Móðir."

Her statement is met with scorn.

"Then you seek death," the man says. "Perhaps the Lang-amma should devour you now. It is a better death than what you'll receive from the Móðir."

"My fate is to die by my husband's side," she replies.

"Your fate? It is to be devoured by the Lang—"

"Still thy tongue, dótturson!" The young woman interrupts, then addresses Auður. "You know your husband's accusers speak the truth. He is what they say he is."

"I care not, Lang-amma," Auður confesses. "I have seen his heart, and it lies with me."

"You are certain of this?"

"I know where he sleeps."

"Interesting." The Lang-amma sniffs the air. "I can smell the stench of his infidelity on your skin. Are you not shamed? You should know, the outcome of what occurs this night may not be what you wish for."

"I wish for nothing more than my husband back," Auður says with conviction.

"So mote it be." The Lang-amma turns to her companion. "This being said, the Móðir and Her cult have become the nuisance we knew they would be. It could well be an opportunity to rid ourselves of the scourge."

He inclines his head. "What do you propose, Lang-amma?'

"Provide this woman with the runes to repel the Móðir from her husband. While the goddess is distracted, we shall eliminate Her cult."

"What of the tithe?"

"There will be more than enough sacrificed to the Vargr to satisfy its hunger, Haraldr Dótturson. Gather the crews. Make ready the dragon ships to sail. If we are to do this, we must do it now, when we have the advantage. The snows this year have been light, and the Móðir will be weak."

"All the weaker, the less She feeds," he agrees. "What of Her progeny?"

"Let me worry about Vánagandr. The Eddas will speak of this day for all time! The night when the Wolf is devoured, and the Mother of Monsters banished!"

Auður interjects with a timid question. "Banished? How?"

"We've waited for this day, planned it for years, and now it is here," Haraldr says. "In recent years, the raiding parties have brought their tithes of coin, salt, and lead; while The Lang-Amma's elite guards have traveled the known world, seeking the tools with which to imprison the Móðir." He gestures to a large, ornamental, stone sarcophagus in the back of the cave.

"This gift, from the priests of Thoth in the Kingdom of Egypt over half a millennia ago when I was attached to a Roman Legionary," the Lang-Amma explains, "was built for the trade of eternal knowledge and lined with thaumaturgical metals. It will hold the Móðir in a prison Lokke would fear."

"But where will you banish Her to?"

"Somewhere over the western sea, past the edge of the world," the Lang-amma replies.

"Yes," Haraldr says. "A far-away place of legend, called *Vinland.*"

8: YESTERDAY

FRIDAY, DECEMBER 13, 2024 3:47 P.M.

WHETSTONE GULF STATE PARK, LOWVILLE, NY

**LAKE-EFFECT EVENT SNOWFALL: 24"
ACCUMULATION (AND FALLING)**

Ethereal in the squall, the headlights of the snowmobiles fight to pierce through the elements. Stu and Jay and their machines persist through the drifts and falling snow, coming to a stop in front of a small, rustic cabin.

The snow has picked up, creating a whiteout. They lift their visors to see and hear each other better.

"I think we're gonna need to stay here for a bit until this shit settles down some!" Stu shouts.

Jay nods. They dismount their snowmobiles, cover them with tarps, and enter the cabin. Stu makes sure to bring his rifle inside.

Just in case, he tells himself. *You never know.*

The interior is Spartan. There's a bunk bed complete with thin, teal-colored mattresses but no sheets or blankets. A table, a pair of chairs, and a kerosene heater, and a small sink complete the amenities .

Stu wastes no time in igniting the heater. Jay pulls a floorboard up, exposing the smuggling drop spot. He stashes their cargo of meth inside, then replaces the board, stomping on it a few times to make sure the fit is tight.

"How long do we want to wait?" he asks Stu.

"A couple hours at least. The weather guy said it should move on to Syracuse later this afternoon," Stu answers

"It'll be getting dark," Jay reminds him.

"I know, but we have headlights and more than enough gas in our tanks. For now, though, it might be nappy time." He withdraws a flask of Jameson's from his pocket and takes a swig before handing it over.

"Might be," Jay says. "I've got the top bunk!" He clambers onto it before Stu can protest and wads his jacket up to use as a pillow. "Penthouse suite, bitches and hos!"

Stu, without the excessive display of vulgarity, climbs onto the bottom bunk.

Within minutes, they are snoring away...

•

*T*he Others, animating the bodies of a bear and a deer, follow the trail left behind by the machines. They move slowly, impeded by the snow's depth. But the eons serving Their cold mistress have taught Them patience, and They know They don't have to run.*

Far ahead of Them, Sbli'rldlnisa-aea floats above the drifts surrounding a small, snow-covered shelter. The elder goddess knows Her prey hides within these walls. She watches with the great, pulsating eye at the center of Her grand bell, gazing into the minds of the wayward men who so brazenly declared 'rings don't fill no holes.'

Of course they don't, *the great goddess of ice and snow acknowledges. A ring is a symbol of faith, a goal to achieve, is it not?*

She sees they are not kind men; they have harmed those they claim to love. She understands they are men who would shield themselves from harm with the bodies of their wives and children.

They will not be missed by those who would mourn them, *She assures Herself.*

No... they would be better served as sustenance for the one who protects Her flock. After all, will the sacrifice of these evil men not allow the protector of this land to flourish?

When The Others finally arrive, Sbli'rldlnisa-aea rises over the roof of the cabin, engulfing it in Her majesty. Her tentacles spread, while tendrils extending from the hydrostatic skeleton of Her trunk slip through cracks in the building's frame. They slither and seek the bodies of its occupants...

And find one.

•

ason Nichols' dreams are not what he expects, laden with horrors no sane person could see without going mad. His eyes are closed but they are active under the lids, darting left and right, up and down. They are watching something deep within his subconscious.

He sees skeletal creatures moving through snow and darkness, grinning with white teeth and exposed mandible bones. The creatures are singing in a language he doesn't understand.

'Sbli'rldlnisa-aea, Gudinnen av alle ting.'

'Sbli'rldlnisa-aea, For himmelens droning.'

The deepest parts of his brain know his fear. It's innate, all consuming. On his bunk, his body sweats and shivers, a reaction not only to the cold, but to the nightmares he is enduring within the dreamscape of his psyche. He listens to the words of the song and gradually comes to understand them.

The Goddess of all things...

Yes, my Goddess.

Jay recalls the woman from the bar. She wanted him, not Stuart. Who was he to come between them?

He knows where she is. She's in the cabin with them.

But She has come here for me, not him!

Lust fills his body. His cock engorges, seeking to enter his new love and bring them together as they were meant to be. As one.

Then She comes into view... floating above him, raven hair fluttering in the air. No longer clothed, She's even more beautiful nude, a perfect body, with no imperfections. She's an angel... *HIS* angel. And he knows She will lay with him, not that Goddamn Stu. He opens his arms to embrace his new Goddess.

She falls into him and accepts his offer.

•

SOMEWHERE ELSE...

The music inside the Hill-N-Dale bar is deafening, but Jay doesn't care. He's elated to be here, banging his head, although he's not certain how it happened. Moments before, he was sleeping in a cabin in the woods, a full-on, hard-on fantasy about the hottie they met earlier going strong.

And now?

He's back in the bar. It's all the same, except the population has increased. The building is filled with patrons dancing or drinking. Katie's there, her prude-ass busily serving.

Hey, sugar. A woman's voice reaches his ears, cutting through the wall of sound. He remembers her, *'Sandy, but you can call me Bella,'* as she told him and Stu earlier.

Never mind how Jay got here, how did *she* get here? Shit, where did everyone come from? He sees folks from all walks of life frolicking about, but the only people he recognizes are Katie and Bella. The band is playing a song he doesn't know, but the lyrics bring him a strange déjà vu.

Little white lies

They caused the tears you cried

And washed away all the feelings

You had inside

For me and anyone else...

The lead singer's hair thrashes, his neck vibrating with each breath as the words flow out. An Indian woman stands in front of him, singing along.

Only time will heal the pain

That caused your heart to die!

The singer arches his back as the last, sustained note rings out.

Sing it like you mean it, karaoke-rock-band-man! the Indian woman declares.

This song is about a husband who cheated on his wife. I think it's very sad, Sandy-but-you-can-call-me-Bella says. *Don't you?*

Jay doesn't answer; instead he has a moment of clarity as a familiar voice breaks through the music.

JAY? ARE YOU IN THERE?

It's Stu. But he's not here. Jay frantically searches for his friend, but he's nowhere to be seen. *Where's Stu?*

Panic is starting to set in. He shouldn't be here. None of this should be happening. He should be in a cabin, with Stu, sleeping and waiting out the storm.

JAY?!?!

The singer in the band doesn't care, belting out the chorus:

No lack of love, baby

Just a lack of trust so maybe

We should call the whole thing off

And find out what we lost...

The song continues, but Jay isn't listening to the lyrics anymore. *STU!* he shouts, but his words are drowned under the music.

Don't worry, lover. Stu will be with us soon. Sandy-but-you-can-call-Me-Bella's sultry voice invades Jay's brain.

Everyone in the bar turns and looks at him while the band breaks down into a bridge:

Time can't tell what you say or do,

Don't tell me I don't think about you.

What we've done it's on our own

We've tried so hard, I guess we'll never know.

No, we'll never know…

A guitar solo shreds. Jay runs to the door and pulls on the handle, but it doesn't move. A kaleidoscope of lights flashes and strobes, and laser beams of colors come to life. The music's volume increases as the lights build in intensity.

Through the fogged and frozen window, Jay can see Stu, standing in the cabin. Frantic, he pulls harder on the handle, but the door still refuses to budge.

JAY! Stu mouths from the other side.

But Jason can't hear him. A hand rests on his shoulder. He knows who it is without having to turn around.

Sandy-but-you-can-call-me-Bella's reflection in the glass obscures Jay's view of Stu.

No lack of love, baby

Just a lack of trust so maybe

We should call the whole thing off

And find out what we lost...

What we lost... what we fuckin' looooooooost!

The singer carries the last note out as Sandy-but-you-can-call-me-Bella wraps her arms around Jason Nichols, and he feels her all over him... all throughout his being ... as he becomes one with his lover.

He closes his eyes and fades away with the music...

•

Something drips onto Stuart Hinds' forehead, waking him up from his nap.

Did Jason piss the bed? he wonders as he wipes his face.

Expecting to find liquid, he instead discovers a viscous slime.

What the fuck?

He opens his eyes to a soft, neon glow coming from the top bunk.

"Jay?" He gets up to look, expecting to find Jay watching a video on his phone, or something.

What he sees is shit more fucked up than he could ever imagine. He's not even sure where Jay actually is. A cocoon of coiled, pulsating, color-changing tendrils in a puddle of black goop occupies the space where Jay should be.

"Jay?" Stu manages. "Are you in there?" He's not sure of anything better to say.

When there's no response, he grabs his rifle and pokes the cocoon with the barrel. It's solid, and resists the pressure by coiling tighter and glowing brighter.

"This is fucked up. What in the hell is going on?" Stu goes to the cabin door, thinking maybe Jay stepped out for some reason.

And left a glowing multicolored tendril cocoon?

He shoves the thought side and opens the door. The expected snow is there, but Jay is not.

The unexpected, however, is also there.

"You've got to be fucking kidding me." Stu says, seeing a familiar bear and deer. Dead, but not dead, and looking right at him. He slams the door shut.

A dream? he suggests to himself, but he's not buying the bullshit.

The tendrils seem quiescent, allowing him time to gather his wits and determine his best course of action is to get the fuck out of here.

He hastily suits up, and is almost finished when something pokes at his chest.

What the hell?

Looking down, he sees a tendril wavering in front of him. He instinctively swats at it with a tattoo-covered hand—

And is jolted by a spark of electricity, accompanied by a mind-ripping screech.

A split-second later, the cabin's kerosene heater explodes, somehow ignited by the galvanic discharge. Stuart Hinds is blown backwards through the open door, rifle still in his grip. He lands headfirst in a snowbank and wriggles about to orientate himself as flaming debris falls all around him, lighting up the night.

The dead-but-not-dead bear and deer are nowhere to be seen, presumably hurled away by the blast, if not destroyed. But what's weird is the sky. It's pulsating with colors, as if an aurora borealis were in full effect, but only over this spot.

"The fuck *is* this?" Stu yells, plowing through the snow toward his Polaris.

A snowbank ahead of him lurches, and he hears a guttural, bestial roar. The dead-but-not-dead bear bursts from the snow. Nearby, the antlered head of the dead-but-not-dead deer does the same.

Stu shoulders the .30-.06 and fires until it's empty. There's no fanfare, only the muzzle-flash and loud report. Panicked though he is, his aim is true, as both undead animals go down. Bone shatters, pieces of antler, teeth, and skulls, flying.

It takes all eight shells to make them stop moving, but it works.

Unsure if they'll rise back up anyway, Stuart drops the gun and hauls ass to his sled. He's not dressed for it, not wearing a hat or gloves, but being anywhere *not* here is a far better option for survival.

He speeds off into the wilderness, looking back once to see an unnatural light filling the spot where the cabin once stood. Right now, Stu's only thought is to put as much space as he can between him and whatever the pod person fucking thing that was.

He'll regret this later as more snow falls, and the winds pick up…

9: NOW & THEN

NOW...

FRIDAY, DECEMBER 13, 2024 4:27 P.M.

WHETSTONE GULF STATE PARK, LOWVILLE, NY

LAKE-EFFECT EVENT SNOWFALL: 28" ACCUMULATION (AND FALLING)

Sbli'rldlnisa-aea roars in pain as She moves to touch the prey... and Her embrace is forcefully rejected. A searing pain courses through Her being. She's not known such agony since being captured and brought to this place, an eon ago. The Others feel it, too, and are stunned by the shock. The *impact the prey's weapon has on Their host bodies forces them to retreat.*

Then She sees ancient wards of protection cover the prey's skin, crafted by the priests of the All-Father, and of Her nemesis, the thunder god Þórr.

To face the thunder god is to face death. The Great Goddess of Ice and Snow's memory is as infinite as time itself.

Oh, She remembers. How can She forget?

Forget how Auður, Þórr's witch, used these same wards against Her? When the scars still mark Her tentacles from that fateful night, her personal Ragnarok? Yes, She remembers it all very well, the Lang-Amma and the death...and how She came to be here.

•

THEN...

STÖÐ, ICELAND, 806 A.D.

A full moon fills the night sky, while thunder roars and lightning sprouts from black clouds above the volcanoes of Iceland. Beneath this spectacle, within a gorge, the cultists of Angrboða are gathered. Carrying torches, covered in white robes, they surround the priestesses of their Great Goddess of Ice and Snow. Ahead of them is the mouth of a massive cavern. Smoke and mist rise from it, mixing with the falling snow.

"Sbli'rldlnisa-aea, Gudinnen av alle ting." The worshippers sing, evoking the true name of their patron deity in the chant. *"Sbli'rldlnisa-aea for himmelens droning..."*

A bound man is carried on a litter, naked but for the ropes binding him, and the hood covering his head. He is the honored sacrifice who has imbibed Heidrun's mead, preparing him for his fate to become one with the Móðir. All sacrifices must come with pain, otherwise they would not be a sacrifice.

Auður follows the procession, cursing the cultists as she weeps and wails. "He is my husband! Only I should be his judge, not any of you!"

She is ignored.

"Alföðr, hear me!" Auður shouts, desperate.

Those nearest to her stop chanting. They turn, bend, pick up bits of volcanic rock, and throw them at her.

She covers her face, but the rough edges cut and scratch her hands and arms. She falls to her knees. "Save my husband from these monsters! Óðinn!"

A crack of thunder from a distance is the only reply. One of the cultists pulls back her cowl, revealing Hilda Bjornsdottir's teary-eyed face.

"Why are you interfering, Auður?" Hilda says. "Your husband lied to my Freydís, laid with her on many occasions; told her he would care for her. Now she is with child, and he pretends innocence? How can you be so devoted to such a man?"

"You speak of lies? *Those* are the lies! He's done no such thing!" Auður protests. "*Your* daughter—"

"*My* daughter has been wronged! Ólafur's faithlessness is well-known, yet you refuse to see the truth. His sacrifice will further our prosperity under the Móðir. At least then, he serves some purpose"

More thunder rumbles. Auður thrusts an arm skyward as if it is an omen. "May Þórr smite you with his hammer!"

"Þórr isn't here," Hilda says. "We stand in the glory of Her Greatness, Angrboða the Móðir, beloved consort to Lokke, with whom she birthed Hel, Fenrisúlfr, and Jǫrmungandr." She hurls another rock, then spits at Auður for good measure.

"You'll learn! You'll all learn!" Auður shouts after Hilda as she rejoins the procession. "Óðinn and Þórr will hear my cries, and bring justice!"

At the mouth of the cave, cultists light torches lodged in its stone crevices. The wind and blowing snow do their best to extinguish the flames, but fail. The litter bearing Ólafur is set down. Circling it, they resume chanting.

"Sbli'rldlnisa-aea, Gudinnen av alle ting. Sbli'rldlnisa-aea For himmelens droning."

More thunder rolls. Furious lightning dances in the black clouds. Smoke pours from the volcanoes. A bank of fog rises.

Then, eerie lights glimmer in the mist. The chanting grows louder, more fervent. The thickening fog parts as it nears the sacrificial litter.

A comely, nude woman with long dark hair emerges from the cave. She is oblivious to wind and cold, walking through the snowy accumulation with ease.

The cultists bow their heads, their chanting dropped to a hushed communal whisper.

"Móðir…Móðir…Móðir…Móðir…"

The naked woman raises her arms, then spreads them, approaching the litter.

Screaming, Auður pushes through the throng and places herself between the woman and her catatonic husband. From her bosom, she withdraws a sigil, a silver amulet carved in runes and holds it aloft.

The dark-haired woman stops. She tips Her head, curious, extends a hand as if to touch the charm. A violent spark cracks from it, making the goddess's avatar flinch back.

"May Þórr's lightning hold all evil away from Ólafur!" Auður cries, spewing the words with as much venom and disdain as she can muster. "May Þórr protect him with Mjǫllnir! Flee from here, evilness! You get nothing from Ólafur; the gods of Ásgarðr shield him from you. The gods are under him and over him!"

The woman recoils. Several cultists close in on Auður, but any threat is short-lived when a bolt of lightning streaks from the sky, striking the rocky ground between them.

The gods, it seems, have chosen to answer her call.

The blast sends robed bodies flying. Auður, knocked to the ground, rolls and finds herself beside the litter where the drugged Ólafur remains bound in a stupor, oblivious to the chaos.

The Móðir remains standing, although She appears shaken, suddenly uncertain.

"The gods protect us!" Auður taunts, still holding the amulet. Emboldened by it, she rises and advances. The woman shrinks away, retreating, seeking the refuge of Her lair.

Trusting the gods, Auður lunges and presses the amulet to the woman's back. There is another violent spark, far louder and stronger than the first. The woman shrieks in pain, Her eyes wide open, Her mouth agape. Strange light streams out of Her distorted face as Her body writhes.

A shower of arrows blocks out the moon as a wolf's howl fills the night... while the agony of a thousand strikes of lightning sears Sbli'rldlnisa-aea...

•

NOW...

FRIDAY, DECEMBER 13, 2024 5:16 P.M.

WHETSTONE GULF STATE PARK, LOWVILLE, NY

LAKE-EFFECT EVENT SNOWFALL: 32" ACCUMULATION (AND FALLING)

The pain sears Her. It's agonizing and She has never forgotten, not in over an eon. The Others flee their animal hosts, desperate and afraid, returning to Sbli'rldlnisa-aea's embrace. They absorb back into Her majesty, making Them whole again.

Now the Great Goddess of Ice and Snow's rage surfaces, and Her intent is clear. She will devour this mortal and send it to Her version of Hell by any means necessary.

She won't be alone in seeking him. Her adopted flock lives in these hills. They love Her and will aid Her.

After all, is She not their Móðir, the Goddess of all things?

•

THEN...

STÖÐ, ICELAND, 806 A.D.

More arrows, fired by the Lang-amma's warriors, rain from the sky. Their deadly shafts cover the rocky terrain with death, piercing the bodies of fleeing cultists. The lightning from the volcanic storm may not have been sent by the gods themselves, but who is to say it wasn't?

The plan has gone as expected.

Auður, gripping the amulet, smiles in satisfaction as the screeching Móðir vanishes into Her cave. She goes to the litter holding her husband, dodging arrows in the process, and embraces him, kissing his face. Delirious, the drugged Ólafur does little to reciprocate, even when she removes his bindings and urges him to move.

"Come, husband. You are free!" Auður shakes him, cries his name, even slaps him, hoping for some response, but getting none. She tries to lift him, but he is too heavy.

She cries and pounds on his chest with her fists, her frustration growing. Around her, all the cultists are dead or dying, or routed in chaos. As she continues to shake and implore Ólafur, trying to bring him to his senses, a sudden dark and terrible chill falls over her.

A new presence looms in the yawing black mouth of the cave. With a huff, and a low growl, the Móðir's second born steps into the moonlight.

Fenrisúlfr.

The great beast is half-dead and half-living, fangs bared, slime dripping from its jowls. Patches of mangy fur do little to conceal the worms and maggots teeming in its rotting flesh, and the sickly glisten of exposed bones. It is monstrous, an ancient dire-wolf of gigantic proportions.

As it stalks toward Auður and Ólafur with slow and murderous menace, she raises the charm again.

It doesn't stop.

She repeats the words taught to her by the Lang-amma. "Alföðr! Þórr's lightning hold all evil away from us. Þórr protect us with Mjǫllnir. Flee from evilness! The gods are under us and over us."

'No... gods... only... Móðir.' The words of Man come somehow from Fenrisúlfr's fiendish maw; *The Others*, their voices legion, speak through the shell they animate.

Auður's arm and hand shakes as she learns the prayer is in vain. The charm's power has no immediate effect on this... *thing*. Nor do the arrows piercing its moldering hide and plunging into its putrescent body. Its massive paws heedlessly crush the cultists in its path; there is no discrimination in its fury. Feral yellow eyes remain fixed on its prey, lips curled back from its snarling teeth.

Tears stream down Auður's cheeks but she holds firm, standing her ground and brandishing the charm as she, again, invokes the gods. The great undead wolf roars in defiance. Its fetid breath stinks of decay. It nudges her with its horrid muzzle, knocking her off her feet. She lands atop the inert Ólafur.

'*You...fool...you...die...no...Valhǫll.*'

Fresh terror suffuses Auður, who scrambles to put space between herself and the undead wolf. It's a futile effort; a large paw pins the hem of her dress, preventing her from moving. She screams, clinging to Ólafur in another vain attempt to wake him from his drugged stupor.

A flash of lightning strikes, a deafening thunderclap on its heels. The ground shakes, upending the litter, sending both Ólafur and Auður sprawling. She loses her grasp of the charm and is frantic as she attempts to retrieve it and hang it from her neck.

While she's distracted, Fenrisúlfr rears up on its hind legs—

Some vast and unseen force rips the great wolf away from them, flinging it into a towering rugged escarpment. Fenrisúlfr yelps once, as if in surprise. A second time in pain, or what the undead call pain. A third leaks out as a dangling sigh before the beast collapses in a broken heap at the base of the rocky slope.

The lingering distant echo of a howl drifts through the night.

The mists dissipate, revealing a gigantic anthropomorphic being as much human as wolf. Its coat is black, its red eyes stare with hatred at its opponent, crumpled at the base of the hill.

"Lang-amma?" Auður manages tentatively to ask. The creature does not acknowledge her, intent on its gory business.

The dire-wolf thing, one of its forelimbs dangling by a rotting tendon, squirms out of its attacker's grip in an effort to bring it upright. The Lang-Amma stretches out its arms, raises its head, and howls, taunting the dire-wolf. In response, Fenrisúlfr launches at the werewolf without hesitating.

Swatting at the dire-wolf with a clawed fist, the Lang-Amma knocks it to the ground, driving the undead beast's snout into the blood soaked earth.

The Lang-Amma seizes the opportunity and descends upon the stunned Fenrisúlfr in a frenzy of thrashing limbs, gnashing jaws, and tearing claws. Within moments, little is left of mighty Fenrisúlfr, but for a seething mass of sticky black slime, bubbling like tar.

This mass, the essence of *The Others*, squirms and oozes toward the cave entrance, as if somehow sentient and seeking escape. Before it can reach its sanctuary, a group of the Lang-amma's warriors rush in, setting it ablaze with torches.

A thousand thousand voices scream in agony, the voices of *The Others*, those the Móðir had consumed, damned to be part of Her for all time.

Or…until now.

'Móðir! Save us! Móðir! Móðirrrrrrrrrr…'

The screams fade as the flames consume the mass, its blaze a finality *The Others* never feared or anticipated. From *The First*, whom the Móðir first fell in love with, to the most recent, the fire burns and purifies. It frees Their souls from the Goddess's eternal grip.

More warriors approach, some with the eyepieces of their helmets stuffed with cloth to block their vision, some with their heads covered in sacks. Armed with axes and spears and shields, they form a semi-circle around the mouth of the Móðir's lair, cutting off any surviving cultists from gaining access.

They raise their shields and slap them with their weapons, shouting out as one, "Skål!"

In response, the Lang-amma roars in triumph, leaps over their line, and plunges into the cave with wild abandon.

A few men carry between them a coffin held aloft by long poles. This, they set down near where Auður sits beside Ólafur.

Who, finally, stirs and rouses, much to her joy.

"Husband!" she cries, embracing him.

He shakes his head, still groggy. "What...what have you done, woman?"

"I've saved you!"

"*Saved* me? You stupid cow!"

"You...why ... ?" She blinks at him, confused.

"I gave myself to the Móðir!" Ólafur pushes her away from him.

"To that ... that thing? Why? Oh, my love, what's—?"

"Love?" He sneers. "With you? I want nothing to do with you! Becoming part of the Móðir's consort is something I've long sought. But *you*, you had to *ruin* it!"

10: TODAY & THEN

TODAY...

SATURDAY, DECEMBER 14, 2024 12:35 P.M.

THE TUG HILL, REDFIELD NY

LAKE-EFFECT EVENT SNOWFALL: 4' OF ACCUMULATION

In the A-frame, the Hatcher brothers listen to ABBA lament about Fernando and the Mexican Revolution while they wait for their unexpected guest to return from the outhouse. All is fine until the Stereo-8's sound warbles again. It's not like before, when the tape broke. This is...different. The words, the music, are shifting, changing. The voice, no longer Frida's, now brings a sense of Deja Vu.

I know that voice, Aaron thinks. "Joey, you hear what I'm hearing?"

"I do, but, how? Makes no sense."

"Fucked if I know," Aaron replies.

The lyrics are the same, but the voice has changed. The music, too. Instead of the strings, keyboards, and synth drums of the ABBA hit... a bass drum kicks in time with a roaring bass line as electric guitars wail the melody, and a woman's familiar voice screams the vocals, complete with a familiar vibrato.

Sounds like Aunt Bobbie. Aaron finds it hard to accept, but it's clearly her voice.

But Roberta Webster, known on the local music scene as 'Bobbie Be Good,' disappeared during the Blizzard of '93. All the searches for her turned up was a boot in a pile of snow.

Aaron goes to the stereo and digs through a stack of compact discs sitting next to an ancient Discman, searching for one in particular.

"What's that?" Joey asks.

"Aunt Bobbie's demo CD. Remember how proud she was?"

"Dude. I was like three years old. All I cared about was Barney. So, no."

"Well, I do. And the song playing right now?" Aaron points to the speakers.

"Yeah? What about it?"

"It's off this CD!" He waves the case held in his fist.

"How's that even possible?" Joey questions.

"How the fuck do I know?" Aaron flops into a chair and leans his head back. "This has been one messed up hunting trip. First the storm, then I see weird lights and hear voices when I'm in the shit—"

"Voices?" Joey interrupts. "You didn't tell me about that."

"Well, I sorta did when I asked if you were pranking me earlier." Aaron shrugs. "Sorry, I was vague, my bad. But now this biker dude shows up ranting about wendigos? And the music? All too weird."

"You've been doing too many edibles. The CD player probably turned on."

"Yeah?" Aaron holds up the cable, which is not connected to the stereo. "I'm telling you, I'm just—"

He is cut off by the television turning on of its own volition. The color tube is shot, and the screen shows a black and white image of a woman singing, her lips in sync with the same tune issuing from the stereo.

"Is that Aunt Bobbie?" Joey asks.

"Holy fuck," is all Aaron can say.

The song ends, and when the next starts, the lyrics and music are as far from ABBA as possible.

"*Sbli'rldlnisa-aea, Gudinnen av alle ting... Sbli'rldlnisa-aea for himmelens droning...*"

The words are foreign to them.

Until they aren't...

"*The goddess of all things... Honyarekowa...*"

The TV flickers, static and digital snow distorting the screen. Nonetheless, through it, they can still see the woman they knew as their aunt. As the camera zooms in, or she moves toward it, her visage is in extreme close up, as if about to press against the glass.

Then it does, and the glass bulges as her head pushes through, musclefollowed by her shoulders, followed by the rest of her.

Dumbfounded, Joey and Aaron can only stare in disbelief as Aunt Bobbie emerges from the television, naked as a newborn.

At this moment, the Hatcher brothers, Keepers of the Old Faith of the Haudenosaunee, finally grasp what is happening. They understand why their long-lost aunt disappeared, where she's been all this time, why she's returned ...   and what their mission is.

Aaron grabs a poker from the woodstove before he and Joey open the door and step outside...

•

THEN...

STÖÐ, ICELAND, 806 A.D.

Auður gapes in shock, unable to believe the words coming from Ólafur. After all she's done to save her marriage, to secure her place in the village? After all she's accomplished on this day?

He... rejects me?

The Lang-amma warned her, but she wouldn't listen. Now, Ólafur gets up, stumbling away from her, showing her his back, ignoring her.

The man she loved.

The man she believed in and fought for.

The man she *saved*!

Before she can fully begin to lament his cruel rejection, The Lang-amma bursts from the cave, bleeding, strangely circular wounds covering Her back and sides. She has a long, severed, purplish tentacle clenched in Her jaws, its ends trailing. As She spits it to the ground and howls victoriously, the warriors cheer, again beating their shields in response.

Behind the Lang-amma, deep within the darkness, an unearthly light blooms, its color shifting and pulsating, growing in intensity.

The Lang-amma turns, teeth bared, fangs dripping with saliva. Auður could have sworn it was an eager grin of anticipation.

Perhaps it is.

The being known to these people as Angrboða, the Mother of Monsters—emerges from Her lair, no longer occupying a human form, but in Her full regalia and eldritch majesty. Gigantic, Her tentacles and tendrils flow like hair from below the dome of Her massive, all-seeing eye.

She is glorious to behold... the very essence of an elder god, and She is very angry.

The warriors cannot see Her; their eyes are covered. They cannot hear Her; their ears are filled with tallow. They've rehearsed their actions for years in preparation, and go about their duty without error.

The Lang-amma, however, has Her full spectrum of senses, nearly being a goddess Herself, and is immune to the charms and glamours of the Móðir. She is the embodiment of the runes carved onto Auður's amulet, those inscriptions protecting the woman from the goddess's glamours, and repelling Her.

A horn sounds from outside the battle, and echoes through the gully. Auður gasps. The earth shakes as the Jarl of Stöð and his personal guard, on horseback, charge in at full gallop. With them is a young woman, dressed in white linens. *Freydís, the stable girl, of course!* A cloudy, violet haze hangs over the throng, and Auður understands why before her husband opens his mouth. *The Móðir. She controls them...*

"They come to aid the Móðir," Olafur says, confirming Auður's assumptions, and spits on the ground. "Perhaps I will get my wish on this day after all."

Another round of thunder crashes and lightning falls from the sky, striking the ground surrounding the combatants. Stone and rock rain on those nearby. The Goddess turns to flee back into the safety of Her lair, discovering Her sanctuary has been compromised. The cave mouth is gone, collapsed under the barrage of lightning.

She is trapped.

In response, with a threatening snarl, the Lang-amma leaps, powerful hind-quarters propelling the werewolf at Her foe. She lands on the Elder Goddess's ocular dome, digging Her claws into the rubbery flesh of the Móðir's mantle. The elder thing twitches and sways, swatting with tentacles, attempting to shake the attacker off.

It's all for naught.

Pieces of the Móðir rain down on those unfortunate to stand below. The warriors present, Auður and Ólafur, all are covered in slimy ichor and translucent pieces of the elder thing's flesh. Tentacles and tendrils whip around, knocking over warriors in attempts to dislodge the shape-shifter from Her being.

None of it works.

The Old One screams... *for help*. Its pitch is high, out of the aural spectrum for humans. The elder goddess sways as gravity takes hold and pulls Her down. Another trumpeting horn blast answers the Móðir's call. She pulses and shrinks, taking on the form of a woman and skulks into the shadows, hiding.

The Lang-amma howls, a hideous, taunting laugh underlining Her call. She leaps to the side and lands in the bloody mud on all fours, then sits, waiting...

The Jarl and his equestrian entourage charge, coming to their goddess's aid. They are dressed for battle, wearing their raiding armor and shields. But the Lang-amma is ready. Auður recognizes them, all former friends, the men who arrested Olafur. At the front of the column are Áki Jónsson and Halfdan Fisker, their axes held out and ready to strike at the Lang-amma.

The Lang-amma cares not. She springs forward, tucking Her forearms into Her chest, folding the werewolf's body into a ball of fur. She lands between the lead horses, an organic cannonball of muscle, fangs, and teeth. The impact sends them flying to either side, ejecting their riders. The next riders rear their reins back, stopping the horses in place, before they, too, are thrown from their mounts.

Claws shred through leather and chainmail. Teeth gnash and rip flesh. A misty fog with a crimson sheen grows as men scream for mercy. None is given. The last man standing is the Jarl, defiant to the end, "Argr seiðr-kona!" he says, cursing Her for a coward, and spits at the ground before his foe.

"Já!" the Lang-amma responds, then lunges forward and consumes his head in one bite.

The masked warriors under the Lang-amma's command rush in, surrounding the Móðir in Her human form. Naked, She beseeches them to free Her in a language long forgotten. The warriors hear not Her pleas. Instead, they secure the goddess's human avatar in chains of silver, covered in the runes of Óðinn and Þórr... *The Thunders*. Her skin sizzles and burns where the links touch. The avatar trails a wake of smoke as the warriors drag Her in front of the Lang-amma.

The wolf-woman grabs the Móðir by the throat and lifts. The Lang-amma tilts her head to the left, then the right, before roaring at the helpless elder thing.

"Far heill, Angrboða!" She tells it, the words guttural and savage as they come from a mouth not meant to speak the words of men.

"Skål!" The warriors shout.

Auður watches all of this unfold, but cares only about Ólafur, an affliction she will soon regret. He remains by the empty sarcophagus, on his knees, weeping, his hands thrown to his face. Without hesitation, she tears the rune charm off her neck and approaches him. Stumbling through the mud, she trips and falls headlong. The earth tastes of blood and death. She pushes herself back up, and crawls to her husband's side.

They don't notice their company.

"Liar!" Freydis screams, and charges at Ólafur, an axe held high in her hands. Still under the influence of the spiked mead, he doesn't move as his former lover swings the blade at him. "You promised to be with me forever!"

The blow strikes him in the face. It knocks him unconscious and the momentum carries, sending him into the open coffin. The heavy axe slips from Freydis's grasp. Auður reaches for it, but Freydis kicks her away.

"You want to be with him still? I can arrange that!" She rains blows on Audur until her fists are bloody and the bones in her fingers are mangled. Once satisfied with the damage she's inflicted, she roars in bittersweet victory. Freydis wraps her hands around Audur's throat and slams her head against the sarcophagus.

Barely conscious and partially blind, Audur attempts to wriggle free from Freydis's assault. With a valiant, herculean effort, she breaks free, only to fall in, following her husband into the coffin.

"This is good!" Freydis Hildasdottir shouts. "He wanted to be with his goddess? I grant his wish! You both will be with Her forever, and I will keep his child and name it after him to spite you. And you? Your memory will be erased from our history!"

Auður arches her back up and thrusts her broken hands out of the coffin, her fingers bent and twisted like tree limbs in winter.

The Lang-amma ignores her pleading gesture and dumps the Móðir's inert body into the coffin with Audur and Ólafur.

"*Tiunda!*" The Lang-amma growls.

The warriors slide shut the cover of the sarcophagus, eclipsing those inside within total darkness.

Auður hears them seal it. She embraces her husband and feels the cold of the Móðir's flesh on her own. She knows her fate, that she is damned.

But she cares not, as the part of her that is still rational knows soon they will be part of the Móðir, that she will still be with Ólafur...

Eilífr.

•

SOMEWHERE ELSE...

Inside the Hill-N-Dale, Stu Hinds listens to the band, and eats chicken wings with Jay Nichols.

A guy, and a woman Stu doesn't recognize, are with them at their table, The guy's a hulking dude with long hair and a thick beard. The woman's a blonde, holding the big guy's hand. Behind the bar, Katie Zimmerman pours pints.

Stu's head throbs, and he's not sure why. The last he recalled, he was in an outhouse, miles from the Hill-N-Dale.

"*Who's this?*" he asks, pointing to their companions.

"Oliver and Audrey," Jay replies. *"They're the first regulars here."*

"Been coming here for years," Oliver says.

First regulars here? But he and Jay have been coming here for years too, and Stu doesn't recall ever seeing them before.

"Yeah, seems like forever." Audrey smiles and looks Stu up and down. A puzzled look covers her face, slowly transforming into one of revelation. *"Look who it is, Olly!"*

"Holy shit! Blood of my blood. I knew eventually you'd come!" Olly embraces a startled Stu. *"My many-times grandson?"*

"Yes! Thank The Mother!"

Grandson? Stu's grandfather died fifteen years ago. *"What's going on?"* Stu wonders, not realizing he's speaking aloud. His answer comes in the form of a fresh drink appearing before him.

"From Bella," Katie tells them.

Stu looks down the length of the bar and sees their benefactor. He slides off his barstool to approach her, but Oliver restrains him with a hand on his arm.

"Hold on a second, grandson," Oliver says. *"She said you'd be here sooner than later, and*

she didn't lie. But you'll need to stay down here for now."

"Yeah, stay down here," Jay affirms.

"Why?" Stu challenges. *"You think she's going home with any of you tonight?"*

"Hah hah! Hardly!" Jay laughs. *"Nope, you're all she wants right now. But she needs to take care of something first. Just eat your wings and enjoy the band."*

The music resonating off the walls seems to agree.

"Yeah, yeah. I get it," Stu says, getting up anyway. *"I've got to use the pisser.*

Then he remembers... isn't Jay dead? Didn't he leave him behind in a cabin twenty miles from here? How did...?

"Of course you do," Jay replies, grinning.

"We'll be waiting for you right here, buddy, right where we've always been," Oliver says.

Stu wonders what the hell that's supposed to mean as he makes his way to the men's room. Finding it empty, he unzips his weather-wear and is about to get down to business when ...

"Remember me?" a woman asks from behind him.

He'd know that voice anywhere. It belongs to Bella.

"How could I forget you?" Stu says. It's not easy to be suave in these circumstances, but he gives it his best shot.

"Then why do you run from me?"

"Oh, I'm not going nowhere, baby."

"Take your clothes off," she tells him.

"Huh? Here?"

"Where else?"

"Don't we want some privacy?"

"It's private here," she purrs.

Stu isn't about to argue further. He pulls his snowsuit off, then hesitates, feeling a cold dampness build on his brow.

"Don't stop," Bella murmurs. *"Take it all off, baby..."*

But something isn't right. He's disoriented, dizzy, as if his inner-ear is out of sync with the rest of him. Everything seems to be turning upside-down.

The pressure in his head flares exponentially. The world blurs around him, as if he's being sucked out of the Hill-N-Dale's men's restroom ... and dumped back into a reality filled with cold and pain...

DEDWADOÑT

11: TOMORROW

TOMORROW...

SUNDAY, DECEMBER 15, 2024 7:00 A.M.

THE TUG HILL, REDFIELD NY

LAKE-EFFECT EVENT SNOWFALL: APPROX. 4'+ OF ACCUMULATION

Stuart Hinds opens his eyes, unsure of how long he's been unconscious. He sees the snow has stopped falling, bits of blue sky and sunlight peeking through the branches of trees. His head throbs and his nose is filled with snot, and though his face is freezing, the rest of his body is numb.

It takes him a few moments to work out why, and when he does, it only brings on more questions.

He's naked, hanging upside-down from a length of rope tied around his ankles, his tattooed arms dangling. He can't move them, and when he tries to speak, to scream for help, he finds he's been gagged.

Suspended nearby are a row of deer carcasses, which helps him remember the cabin and figure out where he is, but doesn't do his state of mind much good.

It does his state of mind even less good when the inverted visage of a deer skull moves into his line of sight, its eye sockets aligned as if staring right at him. As if that's not startling enough, when the skull starts to speak, he loses his shit.

"Sbli'rldlnisa-aea, Gudinnen av alle ting."

Stu would yell if he could, seeing its bare jawbone moving, teeth clacking. The wind briefly swivels him toward one of the carcasses, this one not yet skinned.

It also looks at him, and speaks.

"Sbli'rldlnisa-aea for himmelens droning."

Stu pisses himself. Given his position, the hot stream sluices over his torso, soaking into his snow-caked beard, and dripping from his face.

The A-frame cabin's door opens, and the two Indians he met earlier appear, dressed for the weather and holding curved antler knives. What their plans are for him—which he's certain must be nefarious—what really freaks him out is the woman with them.

No longer attired in the pumpkin-spice stereotype chic she wore at the Hill-N-Dale, she's naked, and smiling, despite the below-freezing temperatures.

"Good morning," one of them says, Stu can't place his name.

"Found one of our knives on you," says the other brother, who'd called himself Aaron; Stu remembers that much. "Planning to kill us in our sleep, were you?"

Stu struggles to speak, to deny the accusation, but he can't.

"Don't bother," Aaron tells him. "We know everything we need to, now."

"Yeah," the other brother adds. "Seems you're a very bad boy."

Fuck you, redskin! The words are clear to Stu's brain, but through the gag he can only make garbling noises. *Joey*, he remembers; *that one's Joey.*

The nude woman stays on the stoop as the brothers advance, the snowpack crunching under their steps, the one called Joey reaches

Stu first and holds him still, as Aaron gets into place for the delicate job he has ahead of him...

The icy numbness affecting Stu's limbs does nothing to settle his nerves. He knows what they're planning to do. They're going to flay him, just like they did the deer.

Only, the deer probably weren't alive and aware as it happened..

Aaron starts at Stu's feet, slicing into the epidermis around his ankles. The cut fully encircles both legs. He then makes long shallow incisions along his calves and the backs of his thighs.

A warm, coppery liquid mixes with the urine, pattering red instead of yellow into the snow.

That's blood, Stu thinks. *My blood.*

Aaron peels the skin from the left leg first, then the right, and bunching the loose folds near Stu's groin.

"Guess you won't be needing these anymore," Joey says, severing Stu's cock and balls with one cut of his antler knife.

Stu hears them land with a wet plop in the snow, and discovers, though he is unable to feel or speak, he can still cry.

DEDWADOÑT

Joey holds him still as Aaron goes to work on Stu's back, neck, and arms. Practiced as he is, it doesn't take him long; he shucks off and tosses aside what is now nothing more than a tattoo-covered shirt of skin. Satisfied with his handiwork, Aaron moves a few paces away to inspect it. His brother joins him.

"Dedwadoñt, Honyarekowa," Aaron Hatcher says, in the tongue of his Grandmothers and Grandfathers before gesturing to the flayed man, their offering hanging from a rope.

Joey Hatcher says the same words, but in the language of the Yankee Colonizers. "Eat with us, great serpent goddess."

Sbli'rldlnisa-aea, still wearing the skin of Roberta Webster, needs no further invitation. The avatar's mouth opens, stretching wider than humanly possible.

Her preternatural roar is followed by an eruption of tendrils, which embrace the skinless body as only a lover can.

Helpless, Stu wants to scream but can't. He dissolves as the tendrils consume his flesh and bone. He. His mind cries out as the Goddess of All Things absorbs him entirely.

But he won't be alone

The Others will be there with him...

Forever.

ACKNOWLEDGEMENTS

This book was not supposed to be a book, let alone a story, nor was it intended to be the sequel to Bella's Boys. Nope. It should not exist, yet here we are, with it in your hands. Look at that sexy cover by Matt Seff Barnes! Yeah, that's Bella as Sandy on the cover...

You see, the sequel to Bella's Boys was supposed to be a joint sequel to both Bella's Boys AND The Death List. The books already had a connection, through Ronnie Dark's made-up band, The Dark. The idea I had developed was for Ronnie to be kidnapped by Bella, and Patrick is tasked by St. D'Inana to save him from the rival Elder God. I may still take this path and tell this story.

Then Dan Henk asked me if I might have a cosmic horror story last year. Taking advantage of the opportunity to share pages with Jeff Strand, Christine Morgan, and other notable talents, of course I said yes. It was on the cusp of a major snow event near me, where the Tug Hill was hit with nearly four feet of snow in a twenty-four hour time period.

Yes. I said FOUR feet.

I explain lake-effect snow often in my fiction (including this book!), I don't think I have to go through the lesson on it here. However, many people don't understand what it is, so here we go, with Wikipedia's definition: *Lake-effect snow is produced during cooler atmospheric conditions when a cold air mass moves across long expanses of warmer lake water. The lower layer of air, heated by the lake water, picks up water vapor from the lake and rises through colder air. The vapor then freezes and is deposited on the leeward (downwind) shores.*

Take my word for it when I say this makes life miserable for me and my neighbors. But I digress...

So, back to this book and its inception! I'm a foodie, and my wife and I eat out frequently, with one of our favorite breakfast spots being on the Onondaga Nation reservation, a restaurant called Firekeeper's. When you walk into the place, the first thing you see is a sign, written in the Onondaga language: Dedwadoñt. And the translation "Eat with us," has stuck with me since I first saw it.

It's not difficult to find a connection between this phrase and the over-used, and racist as fuck, Wendigo trope we see in fiction. But, since my job is to unfuck and correct bullshit of this nature, I set out to write an anti-Wendigo story. Of course Bella was the perfect candidate for the supernatural element in this, especially considering the connection to the Haudenosaunee I'd already established in that book; and further enforced by the Bella's Boys adjacent scenes in SummerHome.

In researching, I learned the Haudenosaunee don't have a Wendigo-like monster in their supernatural repertoire. They've got flint-skinned giants, stone throwing demons, and of course the Flying Head, which I reference in SummerHome and in my forthcoming SummerHome sister piece, WHIRLWIND.

Sticking with Bella's Boys theme of my characters all being "real" people from our world, I decided to make my protagonists Onondagas. They are based off my Magic: The Gathering pals Joe Hatcher and his brother Aaron Webster. I based their cabin off my Dad's work buddy's from back in the day. K-Rod was his name, and he had a pet goat, and it lived on his A-frame cabin. I may actually include K-Rod in a piece as an avatar of Odin... and the cabin is Valhalla... can you say Heidrun?

The antagonists are the "it's all gone wrong" versions of two outstanding individuals in the splatterpunk/extreme horror community (I'm looking at your epic beards, Stuart Bray and Jason Nickie!). I made them in to the exact opposites of who they are in real life. Stu and Jason are the kindest people, so I made their horror counterparts awful humans.

The side plot of Katie, Doc, and Chris is for my buddy Sean (the inspiration for Sean Spencer in SummerHome), a reflection of what he's gone through the past year. Hey, we needed more bodies in this, what can I say? The Hill-N-Dale is a real location, however it's closer geographically to my fake town of Tinker's Falls in real life.

I want to thank Dan Henk for believing in me and publishing the first version of this story in THE JOKE IS ON MANKIND. As soon as I finished it, I knew I wanted to expand on the story.

To Ms. Christine Morgan—I've told you this before, and I will repeat it here. I cannot express how grateful I am for your editing work on this expanded edition of the story. You took a piece that was already good, and made it something next level. People, there's a reason this woman is the first lady of extreme horror. Plus, she knows Norse mythology as well as I do.

I hope you all enjoy your return to the world of my Elder Goddess, and my mash-up of Norse and Haudenosaunee mythology. Bella is one of my favorite creations, and I wish to revisit her again, sooner than later. Until then, the snow is falling... brew a hot beverage, wrap up in a blanket, get a bowl of venison stew, and bundle up with a good splatterfolk book.

Thomas R Clark—DECEMBER 2025

ABOUT THE AUTHOR

Thomas R Clark is a journalist, musician, and author. He is the author of the 2021 Splatterpunk Award Nominated stories BELLA'S BOYS, published through Stitched Smile Publications, and THE GOD PROVIDES, from St. Rooster Books. He is currently the Senior Columnist at Memento Mori Ink. His journalism has appeared in Rue Morgue, This Is Infamous, and House of Stitched Magazine. Tom lives in Central New York with his wife and their canine companions.

9 798999 109156